MANGLED HANDS

A Story of the New York Martyrs

NEIL BOYTON, S.J.

1926 DUST JACKET

TO THE

PAUL BOYTON, JUNIORS

MANGLED HANDS

Chapter One

Little Spoon

I AM TARCISIUS Tandihetsi. My father is Eustace Ahatsistari and he is a captain of our people. That is, he was chief, for he is no more. He has gone to God. I will tell you all. You must know we were forty in twelve canoes. We had seen wonderful things in the Great Villages of the French and we were on our way back to my country. When the sun would be overhead we should come to the mouth of the River of the Iroquois. Then the dangers would be greater. I was not afraid, for I am a Huron and we are brave people. But now like my people I kept my eyes on every wooded bank as we paddled near the silent shores of the Great River. For our enemies are like the poison snakes. They strike and then you see them. I could do this watching easier than paddling, for I am not a man yet. I am a boy of twelve and not large.

It was good to be in this canoe. We were just four and much baggage for the Mission. In the bow was Bernard Atieronhonk. He is my cousin and so are his three sons. He would paddle, paddle for hours and never say one word. I think he prays. He is holy, though he is only a catechumen and has not yet received Saving Waters.

My father, Eustace, as is right for a Huron captain, had stern paddle. He is brave as a she-bear with soft cubs. I like my tall father with his black hair furrowed and ridged as is our Huron custom.

1

He is the handsomest of the fighting men in my village of Te-anaustayae. Catherine, who is his squaw, says I look like Eustace when he was a boy, and if I be good I will be tall as a pine too.

Those were two in my canoe. Right behind me, paddling not as skillfully as Bernard and Eustace, was my other father. He is not Huron blood like we are. He is not even of our blood, for he comes from the land of the French across the Great Lake. I am very glad he did come many leagues to our village last year. The other French want to barter for our beaver peltries. They come with long arquebuses and they are very quick to make them speak. But not so is my other father. He has no thunder-stick, but a breviary hung about his neck and a long black gown which is much worn. He came to tell us Hurons of the land we come to when we go to God. He is a Blackrobe and we Hurons call him Ondesonk. But I call him my other father. For he it was who poured Saving Waters on my head last year and took away my pagan name of Little Spoon and gave me my Christian name, which is the name of a brave boy like me, who went to God many, many, many moons before even the palefaces came into our land.

I was the one who helped my other father to learn our language. It was easy for me to speak Huron. I always knew it even from the days when I was a beady-eyed papoose and Catherine, my father's squaw, carried me strapped to her back. That was long ago.

My other father likes me better than any of the other boys in our village. That is why he asked Eustace to let me go down to the Great Villages of the French, that they call Three Rivers and Quebec, when it was time to get the yearly supplies and provisions for the Blackrobes who are in our villages. There I learnt the name the Frenchmen call my other father. It is, in their language, Isaac Jogues. But I like still to call him in my own tongue 'my other father.' And he is. And he likes it.

I was thinking a puzzling thing that a white squaw who rules the virgin girls in the long convent at Quebec had told me. She said my other father was well named Isaac and that she prayed long prayers that when my other father's hour of God's Will came he would be willing and prepared for the sacrifice.

When I think a thing that I do not understand—and there are many things I do not understand after visiting the Great Villages of the French—I always go to my other father and he always knows the answer. He knows more than five pagan medicine men of my tribe easily! Maybe, more than all the Huron sorcerers.

Just as I was about to open my mouth and form the words of question, Eustace spoke to my other father and ordered him to draw in his paddle and rest for some minutes. You know, the Blackrobes are not like us Hurons. They want to and they try to, but they cannot paddle, paddle while the sun goes from east to west. Eustace can and Bernard can. I cannot yet, for I am a boy and I think the Blackrobes are always like boys at the paddles. They tire out and must rest before they paddle again.

So my other father pulled his paddle in and I took it gladly and laid it on the canvas bags of Mission supplies in front of me. I knew within the next minutes my other father would answer my question.

Blackrobe settled down, stretching his bare feet either side of me. You know, we never wear moccasins in the canoes, for if we did we might bring sand into the birch bark canoes and ruin them. It is not good to find leaks in your canoe when you are many-days' paddling from your villages and enemies on the war path.

When my other father was resting, I leaned back and as his custom was, he put his nice hand that was browned by wind and sun on my forehead and made the Sign down and across.

"Is my Little Spoon weary?" he asked in my tongue, stroking my forehead and drawing me back where I love to lie in the canoe, close to his breast.

"Do not, other father," I earnestly protested.

"Do not what, little son?" asked Blackrobe, again stroking my forehead coolingly.

"Call me by my pagan name unless I am bad. You washed that name away forever when you poured Saving Waters on my head. I am no longer Little Spoon, but Tarcisius, and you are my other father. Am I not a good boy?"

"Always and ever may our Good Lord keep you so," he replied, and his words sounded like a prayer in the Mass.

I was holding his nice hands now. My Blackrobe's hands were long and slender and very perfect. They were brown, not copper colored. There were no hands like them in all our villages. They were not stumpy and hardened like Bernard's and Eustace's, who paddled for many years. It was easy to feel them and I had learnt ever since first my other father came to our villages last year I felt holier for just touching them. I liked to hold them, for I knew they had touched God Himself, and they made me a better boy. This I know always.

So holding Blackrobe's hands while he rested, and Eustace and Bernard paddled silently and the other eleven canoes of our party kept along either side of us there by the shore of the Great River, I remembered my puzzling question about the thing the squaw in the long convent at Quebec had said.

"My other father, tell me one thing and I will be more happy."

"If that were necessary I would gladly tell my small brave two things, would they make him happier. What troubles the mind of little Tarcisius?"

"What did that white squaw who prays all hours in the long convent mean when she said you were well named Isaac. I desire to know."

I looked upwards into the brown bearded face of my other father and he smiled down on me. It is good to see Blackrobe smile, but he does not have time to smile often, and I was not to see him smile many more times.

"You must mean the Ursuline Superior, Mother Mary of the Incarnation."

I nodded, for that was the white squaw I meant.

"Would that I were as pleasing in the sight of the Master as she! I'll tell you what she very likely meant."

Then Blackrobe told me about a Captain named Abraham and his little son Isaac, whose life God wanted back in a very ancient day. I did not understand all that my other father told me, but the telling seemed to make him very happy, for his eyes shone. He is very good to look upon when his eyes shine like brown fires.

Then he said: "Your puzzling question has reminded me of another little Isaac, about whom I once wrote a poem in honor of Our Mother Mary."

Always when Blackrobe begins that way, I know it is wise to listen.

"You will tell it to me now, will you not, my other father?" I asked him, for I know his stories are good to hear. He knows so many stories that we Christian Huron boys like to hear. Even the pagan boys of my village of Teanaustayae listen to him. His tales are so different from those the braves tell, about the cabin fires in the winter time.

"I was Isaac Jogues in those days across the Great Lakes and——"

"How long since?" I inquired, for I like to know all that I may of my Blackrobe's boyhood. It was so strange and interesting and not like mine.

"How long since? I have almost forgotten out here on the Huron Mission. But it must have been fully twelve years ago and that would have been 1630 and I was not yet a poor priest of God."

He fell a-wondering and finally I had to cough.

"I am satisfied," I told him, "Now what about this other little Isaac?"

"Tarcisius will pardon me my day-dreams out here on the bosom of the Great River and I will tell him all at once. I was in my studies and I made my poem from an old legend. It seems in olden days at Constantinople—which is a village larger many times than

Teanaustayae—if there were left some Particles of the Sacred Host, it was the beautiful custom for the priest to call up the little boys and girls and give them the Particles."

"Why should the girls get any?" I wanted to know, for with us Hurons girls are only going to be squaws and keep the fires and they have no rights with boys who will be braves.

"My Little Spoon will have to ask Our Lord some bright day." He smiled down on me and I was silent, for I knew when Blackrobe called me my pagan name I had again carried the Devil in my heart.

But as our Huron custom is, I bowed my head between my knees. This means, I will not do so any more.

I held his nice hands close and my other father squeezed mine and then I knew he had forgiven me. Whenever I have been bad I have but to show I am sorry and my Blackrobe will forget all about it. I think the Good God Who made all things must be that way.

So he resumed as if I had not interrupted:

"One day a little twelve-year-old boy, whose father was a Jewish glass blower——"

I was itching to ask what that was, but I remembered in good time and listened as the gray squirrel does in the high branch when he hears a noise below.

"This son of the glass blower went up with the Christian children and received Our Lord into his heart. When he got home and his father learnt where Isaac had been and what he had done, he was so angry that he opened the door of the furnace, where the glass was melting like ice in the kettle in winter time, and he thrust his son right into the flames."

I thought I knew what happened, for many times, when I was small and Eustace and Catherine were pagans, I have seen our war captives burnt over a fire, and I have helped. I was very bad then and carried the Devil in my breast all day.

But my other father went on: "For three days the little Isaac's mother went about the village looking and looking. She thought surely her son was lost and she prayed God to help her find him. The boy had disappeared as completely as if he had been captured and taken into the Iroquois country to the south.

"Then that third evening the poor mother was praying and in her grief that her prayer was not heard she went about calling her son's name out loud many times, 'Isaac, Isaac, Isaac.' At length she thought she heard him answering. But his voice came from the last place in the world you would have suspected——"

"I know, from Heaven where——" I started to tell my other father, but he corrected me:

"No, Tarcisius mine, that is not the last place, but the first. The poor mother was standing by the door of her husband's glass house. The little Isaac's voice was coming from the midst of the furnace."

"I know then. I have heard captives. Their voice is not nice from the flames."

"But Isaac's was, and the frantic mother threw open the furnace door and saw her little son standing in the very midst of the glowing coals."

"And not roasting?" I had to ask, for that is not the way with captives.

"Not roasting. Isaac came running to his mother's arms and he was as healthy as a certain small Huron chief is."

My other father stroked my head with his nice hands and I knew he did not dislike me. It made me feel so good.

"Naturally all the people in the great village of Constantinople heard of this miracle and when they questioned little Isaac he kept repeating, 'A woman robed in blue, all beautiful, came to see me and gave me water to put out the fire around me and she brought me something to eat when I was hungry.'"

"That squaw in blue must have been God's mother," I told Blackrobe eagerly. "She would do that. I like her always."

"Yes; she was the Squaw in Blue, all beautiful," said my other father, "She always protects her little Isaacs even unto this day."

This made me wish and I complained: "Why did you not give me that name instead of Tarcisius, when you poured Saving Waters on my head last year?"

But Blackrobe smiled as he explained: "Mother Mary's blue robe is broad and she extends it far over all small Hurons who call on her with confidence." My other father's nice hands made a circle over me, lying between his feet in the bottom of the canoe. "Remember this always, little chief."

Here Eustace, my father, asked: "Ondesonk, what did the captains of the Great Village do to the father of that little Isaac?"

"Oh, I forgot that. When the mother and boy received Saving Waters, he refused to have anything to do with them, and the captains punished him for his crime."

I thought over this and then I said: "Other father, they should have burnt him over a slow fire. I would have helped gladly and brought much wood. They should have burnt him to the waist one night and up to the head the next night. I would——"

Blackrobe pushed me from his breast and requested:

"Little Spoon, give me my paddle now for I am rested and must do my share."

I reached it to him and as I did I knew I had said something bad, so I put my lips to my other father's nice hands and pressed them.

He took the paddle and as he straightened into position to ply it, he whispered: "Keep watch on the wooded banks again, for around this bend we begin to come into a dangerous stretch, Tarcisius."

It made me feel good all over to hear my other father call me by my Christian name again. He is the best of all the Blackrobes in my country. I, Tarcisius Tandihetsi, say so.

Chapter Two

Friend or Iroquois?

THE GREAT RIVER ahead was not as wide as it had been last night when we camped on the shore facing the islands in that part which Blackrobe called Lake St. Peter. Now the current against us began to run swiftly even in here by the wooded bank. Soon Bernard Atieronhonk, who had not spoken since we started at gray dawn, trailed his paddle and grunted. Blackrobe and Eustace, my father, kept our canoe motionless in the current. We waited till the next canoe forged abreast. In it were Paul Ononhoraton, Joseph Theondechoren, the old man Ondonterraon, and Charles Tsondatsaa, who is my father's squaw's brother. They were all from my village. None of them, except the old man, are pagans any more. They are all brave, but the bravest is Paul. He should be. He is a chief's son like me.

"Ondesonk," said Eustace, "beyond this bend begins the rapids where the two canoes on the way down to Three Rivers were wrecked."

"We must not repeat that disaster, then," Blackrobe replied. "We lost the letters for France there. Thank God, we lost no good Huron lives. I remember the rapids did not seem half so difficult as others we shot. The surface was broken only in ripples."

"But it was as treacherous as nine Iroquois," Paul put in, and I saw him eying his arquebus, which rested within arm's length on top of more Mission bundles. He is the best shot with bow or arquebus in our village.

9

More of our canoes had paddled up and in one of them were the white braves, René Goupil and William Couture, who are not Blackrobes but help them in the missions. Couture had an arquebus and so had René Goupil.

"Do what Eustace says," ordered Blackrobe, and that was right, for he was captain.

Eustace gave the command for the seven canoes, heavy with the bags of Mission supplies, to go in by the wooded bank and be towed and all the others to paddle ahead.

In shoal water Bernard put the rope over his shoulder and began dragging our canoe among the rocks like a horseman leading his frightened horse by the bridle. Blackrobe and Eustace waded either side guiding our canoe. We were in the lead.

I wanted to help, but my other father objected:

"Small legs are better within the canoe for the next league."

I was glad to crouch low, for lying there I could watch and, better yet, I could rest my small fingers on the nice hands of my other father as he held the gunwale of our heavily loaded birchbark canoe.

Blackrobe smiled down on me often. I was thinking of the Squaw in Blue and asking her to protect us, not from the white waters but from a war party. For the Iroquois in the south countries are the deadly enemies of our people. And Eustace, my father, says they are very dangerous enemies, for they come like foxes and fight like bears and take flight like birds. I have myself seen three braves of our villages who fell into their hands two seasons ago at deer time. They escaped from the Mohawk cantons in the spring, but the three men were not braves any more. They do squaws' work. That is all they are able to do. It is not nice to fall into the hands of the Iroquois. So I prayed to the Squaw in Blue, for I know she is more powerful than many war parties of Iroquois. It made me feel good to think she was my friend. I know this, for Blackrobe has often told me. He is not deceitful like the pagan sorcerers.

When we worked around the bend and could see the next reach of the Great River the matted pine forests on either bank looked to be drawing close together less than a league ahead. Now I remembered the spot quite well. We had camped there the night before we came to Three Rivers and along here I had helped look for the baggage and the packets of letters for the Blackrobes over the Great Lake we had lost when two canoes upset. And I had seen a bear on the bank watching us gravely. They do that sometimes when we paddle past in canoes. I remembered there is a little stream an arrow shot from our camping place where I had caught five excellent trout. Paul Ononhoraton caught nine.

I was thinking of the taste of those fish, when Eustace straightened up and I knew he had sighted something wrong.

We were close in shore and reeds grew thick. Silently he signaled to Paul, who was steersman in the canoe outside us, and that canoe glided up. I saw Paul reach for his arquebus. I had my knife beside me and I could reach it as quickly as a bear can swipe.

Suddenly it was so still that I could hear the roar of the white rapids ahead. Eustace parted the reeds and I saw them wave and then he was not visible. I knew what he had caught sight of. For just beyond where Bernard stood I saw a reed and it had been freshly broken off. Silently I pointed it out to Blackrobe. He did not notice anything wrong about that. I was about to tell him it did not happen itself, when Eustace's head feathers showed. The reeds parted and he was standing in the water by our canoe.

"There is a beach of sand around this point. Come and read the message that is written there."

That was all he said.

The old man Ondonterraon dropped out of his canoe and began to tow it. Bernard and Blackrobe towed ours. They brushed through the clump of reeds that grew into the water and, unnoticed, I followed them. I had my knife with me.

11

The other side of the point was the sandy beach that I remembered. It looked the same as when we camped, but I quickly learnt different.

Eustace and Paul strode across the sand and then stopped. There where the waves ended were the marks of canoes on the wet sands; one, two, three. Where their keels had grated on the sands were the imprints of naked feet. There had been no attempt to conceal them. Paul stooped and examined them carefully. He spoke and pointed out something to my father.

I looked about and I saw that René Goupil and Couture had their arquebuses at the ready and behind them in the tall grasses a score of our Christian Hurons had loosened their bows. It was unbelievably still. Not even a bird was in the sky nor a sound of a squirrel in the dark green forest.

I saw where the water brushed the reeds my other father standing barefooted with his tattered gown tucked up to his girdle and his breviary dangling from his neck. I sidled over to him. He put his nice hand on my bare shoulder. I whispered I felt no fear. I am Tarcisius, a chief's son. Why should I?

Together we looked through the slim reeds and watched Eustace and Paul and others of my people examining the trail. One of these was Charles Tsondatsaa, who is my father's squaw's brother. He had circled around and glided down from the forest. He spoke to Eustace and the two of them disappeared up trail.

Blackrobe saw I was curious to see more, but he pressed on my shoulder and made me crouch down till I was squatting in the water.

"Patience, my little son," counseled my other father, "Whether this is the trail of friend or of our brothers, the Iroquois, the Good God will let us know in His own hour. In the meantime an arrow with its flint point of death might come to the curious. I have known a pussy-cat to have lost nine lives through an over-desire to see too hastily."

I was anxious to hear more about this pussy-cat and I would then have asked Blackrobe, but Eustace and Paul and the other Huron braves came towards us.

Paul spoke: "The trail is not fresh, Ondesonk. It is two-days' old. We agree that there are only three canoes, not more than fifteen men."

"And we are forty with three good arquebuses," put in William Couture, and his dark eyes lit up with that light I have often seen in the faces of brave men who like to fight.

"Of what tribe are they?" asked Blackrobe.

"We do not agree," explained Eustace. "We have examined all the trail to the water's edge. Paul and these," he pointed to Charles and Joseph Theondechoren, "these say the party that camped here are Mohawk Iroquois, but I do not. This is yet the Great River and it is not their season to venture so far. It will be a half-day's journey before we will come to the parts beyond the River of the Iroquois where they might lurk."

"Then you think they are friends?" Blackrobe inquired.

"Allies," Eustace, my father said. "I believe the trail is Algonquin and this party passed down the river last night while we camped on one of the islands in Lake St. Peter. The black night hid their passage from us. They are at Three Rivers trading with the French now. This is my belief, Ondesonk. I, Eustace Ahatsistari, have spoken."

Here Charles Tsondatsaa, who is my father's squaw's brother, spoke: "Ondesonk, the belief of Eustace Ahatsistari is not my belief nor Paul's. This is our belief."

Now all were here at the council in the reeds, except the Hurons on guard in each canoe.

"Speak your belief. We will hear all," ordered Blackrobe.

"There is among the Mohawks of the Iroquois cantons a vile Huron. I know him well. I was a boy with him in our village before the Blackrobes came. When they did, the same day we received Saving Waters on our heads. I became Charles and he was called

James. But he is an apostate and when he was captured one deer time by a band of Mohawks his life was spared and he was adopted into one of their families."

"This is Snake Tooth! Snake Tooth!" said several, and I saw it made them carry the Devil within their breast to remember him.

"Yes; that is his Mohawk name." Charles Tsondatsaa spit it out.

"Is he the one whom the missionaries call 'the man of Maturin'?" asked my other father.

When they nodded, he added: "Poor man! He must be very unhappy within his breast. No one who has had the grace of receiving Saving Waters on his forehead and afterwards rejects that grace can be happy here, and God help him hereafter!"

All affirmed what Blackrobe spoke. I, Tarcisius Tandihetsi, know it is so.

"But I go on with my belief," said Charles, "I know that when the Mohawks captured him, he was tortured in their villages and this toe——"

He stooped over and before I realized what he was doing he had lifted me to his shoulder so that all might see. Then he took my left foot and stretching it out, grabbed the toe next to the little toe and held it tight.

"This toe was hacked off. I have heard it from John Andation of the village of the Immaculate Conception who was taken with him and escaped. It is true."

Again Charles stretched my toe for all to see and when he dropped me to the sands, he finished: "A footmark on the sands beyond the reeds has nine toes and the missing one is the toe I showed you on Tarcisius' foot. It is written many times in the sands. Where this Snake Tooth is, are not our allies the Algonquins, but Mohawks. They are phantoms, these Iroquois, till it suits them to be seen. This is my belief. The trail ahead is not good."

Blackrobe looked at Charles and Eustace and René Goupil. The white brave threw up his hands in the gesture that I have noticed the French traders, who come to our villages for beaver peltries, use when they do not know their own mind clearly.

But Eustace, as he was chief of the party, spoke: "Friend or foe, what does it matter to us? We came down the Great River safely and we must go up it to get to our country. Trust to this trail. We have nothing to fear. If they are Iroquois, however strong they may be deemed, they are not more than three canoes—and their leader is an apostate. They are only a few and we are forty."

"And three arquebuses," again said William Couture. And I could see very clearly that he had the mind to shoot his thunderstick at my vile countryman, Snake Tooth. An arquebus is better than an arrow at a distance, but I do not think it is as good as a war club when men fight close up.

"Eustace speaks wise words," Blackrobe now said. "We must go on. Besides the three arquebuses and many bows, we are in God's Hands. It matters not where we are, provided we rest in the arms of Providence and His holy favor. He Who watches the sparrows, will keep guard over His children of the woods."

"And I have prayed to the Squaw in Blue," I whispered to my other father and he smiled his approval.

So we went back to our canoes and began to tow them in the white water between the troublesome rocks.

When we rounded the point and were towing past the sandy beach with its fresh trail, I slipped out of my canoe and waded ashore to find those footprints. I wanted to see that one of Snake Tooth's. When I found it, I examined it closely, so that I would know it again. But I never thought I would meet with it the way I did.

I wished in my heart that I knew how to shoot René Goupil's arquebus, but I did not say that I carried Devil in my breast when I ran back to my canoe, for I knew my other father would not have called me by my Christian name. As my people did not call that apostate, James, anymore, he would have said Little Spoon. My name is not that ever again, but Tarcisius. I have said it.

Chapter Three

Like a Bear in a Trap

THE GREAT RIVER narrowed until the wooded bank on the other shore came close up and I, Tarcisius Tandihetsi, could tell the trees were white oak, balsam, and much pine. The current was swifter than a Huron runner. I like the roar of the white waters in the rapids. It seemed to me to be saying fast words and I like to listen to them and try and make out their meaning. If I was still a pagan I would believe that the fast waters say words of omen, but I know that it is not right to believe such things. It is very bad and my other father has told me when such pagan thoughts come to say one Hail Mary and the Squaw in Blue will drive them away. I always do and then I find that I think of other things and I know that the robe of grace on my soul, like a robe of beaver fur, is still very beautiful and I am pleasing to God. That is the way I always want to be.

These things was I thinking, lying back against one of the canvas bags that held the Mission vestments, while Bernard, Eustace, my father, and Blackrobe towed our canoe upstream. All three were straining forward as though they were facing a winter wind, for the waters went faster and there were rocks with white collars showing all about our party.

I looked back downstream and could see the eleven other canoes hugging the shore and toiling upstream, strung out like the floats on a fish net. They were all being towed now. It was no place to paddle.

16

Eustace, my father, had just shouted to Blackrobe:

"It is a hard league ahead, but after that the Great River broadens again and soon we will be at the mouth of the River of the Iroquois, when we must be on our guard."

This remark made me look at the rapids we were just entering. The same wooded banks we had seen for leagues and leagues, with the thick tall green trees and now and then an eagle sailing high in the blue sky. You must have keen sight to see an eagle in the morning sky. I saw two at that moment. That is a bad sign. Then I thought to say a Hail Mary and when I was finishing it, saying 'pray for us sinners now and at the hour of our death,' the noise of the roar of the fast waters was driven forever from my mind.

No wonder, for there came from the still green of pines right beside us, and from the other bank, high and long cries with the sharp barks at the end of them. It was the war cry that we Huron boys in our village had used in our games of captives. But I had never heard it given that way by real enemy braves. It is not a nice sound. I dropped low in the canoe.

Then from the nearer bank, where the trees overhung, many arquebuses made their thunder noise. Through the birch-bark side of the canoe right before me a stream of water began to jet over my hand that clasped the knife.

Eustace and Bernard let go the canoe. Eustace fell over me, grabbing his bow and arrows and next second he was hidden in the bank and our war cry, which is deep and strong and makes your heart beat faster, went up.

Bernard Atieronhonk lay across the bows of our canoe, his head feathers dragging in the water, and an arrow was still quivering in the palm of his right hand, fixing it firmly to the canvas bag of Mission supplies. The canvas reddened as he struggled to pluck the arrow out.

Blackrobe blessed himself and labored forward in the fast waters to try and hold our canoe bow on to the current. I leaped overboard to help him, and the water was suddenly up to my breast. So

17

I had to swim a few strokes. The canoe swung broadside and began to drift back on the other canoes. An arrow whizzed by my head and stuck in the birch-bark side of the canoe. Just for an instant I saw downstream and the line of our canoes that had looked like floats on a fish net before, now seemed the centers of white waters and whirling fighting men.

All along the wooded bank we had just passed came war cries, high and long, with the sharp barks that are not nice. René Goupil and the other white brave were standing to their waists in the running waters and firing their arquebuses at the phantoms. For such Iroquois are at the beginning of an ambush.

As the smoke drifted down and hid the white braves' breasts and faces, I saw three of our Hurons, all crumpled up, sinking slowly under the white waters.

Then my other father was shouting:

"Bernard. Bernard."

I looked and, as I did, Bernard with his free hand broke the arrow off close and drew away his gaping palm. He fell back into Blackrobe's arms as the shaft of the arrow came away and I saw there was a gash on his forehead too. I alone was trying to hold the canoe in the current and it was more than I was able, for I am only twelve and have not man's strength yet.

I heard Blackrobe call:

"Bernard, now is the time for your Baptism." And he cupped his hand.

Then I remembered Bernard was not a Christian yet.

I grabbed Blackrobe by his girdle to keep our canoe from being torn out of my grasp and though I could not hear a word he was saying I saw Blackrobe lift his dripping hand and pour Saving Waters on the head of Bernard. I knew he was a catechumen no longer and if he fell in the fight, he would go straight to God.

A frightened screaming bird, maybe a blue jay, for it was not bigger, flew in my face from the bank and I let go my hold on

Blackrobe's girdle, and our canoe now broadside to the white waters began to drag me away. Blackrobe dropped Bernard's shoulder and caught me by the iron anklet on my leg.

He shouted: "Let go. Let the canoe go."

This I did and went completely under water like a beaver. I could still hear the war cries of the Iroquois and our Hurons, but they all sounded a league away, like in a dream fight.

Then as I came gasping up, for my other father had a firm hold on my anklet and it was cutting into my leg, I tried to stand in the fast waters. Blackrobe caught me by the arm and dragged me into the shore, where there were bushes.

I coughed many times for indeed it seemed as if I had swallowed much of the Great River. Only then I discovered what I thought was water dripping into my eye and blinding me, was not water, for when I put my hand up to wipe the drops off, my hand came away all red. I had not known it, but that arrow a few minutes ago must have grazed my forehead. It is this way in the heat of battle. Often have I heard our braves around the cabin fire tell it so.

Blackrobe cried aloud in my ear: "Tarcisius, you and I are not fighting men. So we shall lie low until He Who guards us with ceaseless love decides the battle."

And he made me come with him further into the forest, which was so thick that it was impossible to make much headway. Frightened squirrels barked overhead, but this was not the time to pay attention to them.

Finally, the thick undergrowth thinned. But not till I felt as scratched as though I had fallen into thorns. When I straightened up I saw we had come before a hollow tree that stood stark and shiny. A full-grown black bear was in the act of backing out of a hole that was the height of my hand over my head. Bear's fat is very good to eat, but not at this season of the year.

The black bear scrambled and slid down to the earth. It turned and looked at us, but no fight was in its eye. It dashed into the thickness of the woods beyond this small clearing. It was easy to see that it was a squaw bear and the thunder noises of the arquebuses were not pleasant to her. She must have been asleep when the Iroquois ambushed our party.

Blackrobe made me, though I did not think it brave for a chief's son to do so, climb into the hole and when I turned and peered out, my head was on a level with the opening and through the trees to the bank I could see a little stretch of the shore of the Great River. In the center about a dozen of our Hurons were fighting hand to hand with twice that number of breech-clouted enemies. As I watched I saw our own canoe, deep in the water and abandoned, drift down and strike the first whirling mass of braves. Then it turned completely around in the fast waters and was swept out of my sight. I wished I had taken my knife out of that canoe. It was a good knife that Blackrobe had given me in the Great Village on the Rock.

Most of the fighting Iroquois had dropped their arquebuses and were using tomahawks and knives, that kept flashing in the sunshine. As Blackrobe and I watched, René Goupil and Couture backed into view. Their arquebuses were speaking through much smoke. A tall Iroquois with a red-stained deerskin war bonnet leapt from behind and René went down under his war club. This naked chief of the enemy reached to grab René Goupil's scalp lock and, as he did so, Couture made thunder noises with his arquebus and the red-stained war bonnet of the Iroquois and a part of his head separated right in the sunshine. His painted body fell forward and his hand, with the fingers clutching, disappeared under the white waters. Then three Iroquois leapt at Couture....

When I thought of the tall Iroquois I felt glad within my breast, though I did not say so to my other father, who stood silently all the while at the foot of the bear tree. I knew he was praying. I had forgotten all about my prayers. But, then, I am not a Blackrobe and it was my first battle time.

When I looked again, some Iroquois were dragging the white brave ashore and he slumped and was not able to resist.

"They have captured your companion. I think they have killed him," I cried to Blackrobe.

All he said was: "We are in the Good God's Hands, now as always. Maybe, it is His wish we go down into the south instead of back to your Huronia. Poor René Goupil! I cannot abandon him now."

I did not like to hear my other father utter such words, for we Hurons know it is not good for captives to go down into the lands of our fiercest enemies.

More barking war cries suddenly sounded and, getting up higher in the hole, what next I saw was certainly not good, for coming out of the other wooded bank and swimming and wading across the rapids with their arquebuses and tomahawks held high was a new band of Iroquois, maybe as many again as our whole party.

When I shouted this information down to Blackrobe, he said sadly: "Then the day has gone against us. And many of my poor Hurons are not yet baptized!"

He pulled me down, for in my eagerness to see better I had climbed partly out of the bear hole.

"Listen, Tarcisius mine, and do as I say. Lie low in this hidden place Providence has given you till it is dark. Then try to go down the Great River till you meet with friends or allies who will take you to the villages of the French."

"And are you not coming too?" I asked anxiously.

"That I cannot do. I would be a hireling and no shepherd if I did that."

"But what shall I do," this thought had come to me, "if that squaw bear comes back here before the stars are out? She looked to me as though she had an evil temper and I—I have lost my knife."

My other father reassured me, claiming: "That squaw bear is a league away from this battle field. She will not return."

21

Then he said: "Bend low, Tarcisius."

This I did and he reached up his nice hands and taking my head in them, made the Sign with his right thumb on my wounded forehead.

He again ordered me to crouch in that bear hole and this I promised to do, because I liked him, not because I had fear in my heart.

Then he went towards the bank and, as well as I could, I watched his tattered black gown till my other father had passed out of my sight. And I feared that it was out of my sight forever in this world.

I must have been silently watching for many minutes when, without any sound, there glided under my tree a naked greased Iroquois. He was painted on the cheek in blue and red bars. A war amulet of beads and mole feet dangled from his neck. There was bright red on the studded war club in his hand. Just as silently as he glided, I lowered myself into the blackness of the bear hole.

It was still. For the first time I realized that there were no more war cries and I had not heard an arquebus thunder for many minutes.

I said a prayer to the Squaw in Blue before I ventured to peep again. I saw above the tops of the bushes the bent head of this Iroquois with its three eagle feathers fastened to the black hair. He had discovered Blackrobe's trail to the bank and intently he was following it.

Then it was that I realized for the first time that I was leagues from the Great Villages of the white braves and weeks from the cabins of my own country, and the Mohawk Iroquois, who are our most dreaded enemies, had beaten our party.

It was not good to realize this. I, Tarcisius Tandihetsi, say so.

Chapter Four

The Dawn of Horrors

WHEN THE red and blue barred Iroquois was no more to be seen in the bushes, I came out of that hole in the dead tree as the black squaw bear had done. Only I did not make so much noise. For I knew that it was only a matter of minutes before this Iroquois would cross our trail and trap me in the tree. If he had been a white brave I might have stayed quiet, but we Indians read signs in the woods that the white man never sees.

I struck up the trail the Iroquois had come. Then I saw ahead of me down a lane of leaves a flash of red. I dropped like a bird alights and crawled quickly out of the trail and lay in the bushes still like a doe in the thicket.

It was well that I did for not many minutes later a party of five were passing close by. Three of them were painted Iroquois with war amulets and aprons of deerskin with the red suns painted on them. They carried arquebuses, and war clubs that dripped. They drove before them two whom I recognized with pity. For there, bound with helpless hands, were the squaw Theresa and René Goupil. This white brave walked with weak steps and had been wounded most grievously in the left shoulder.

These had hardly disappeared down the trail to the river bank when another party with seven of our Christian Hurons, all bloody and bound, came along. At first I did not recognize Eustace, my father, for he it was that the captives supported. Heart told me to throw myself into the midst of the captives, but brain said, no, wait.

23

Blackrobe may escape the Iroquois dogs and I will find him and be of use to him.

But I knew now that our whole party had been defeated completely and I wished—if it were not bad to wish so—that Eustace, my father, had gone to God in the trap by the reeds of the river bank. For I would prefer that to what would await him, whom the Iroquois knew was the bravest of the Hurons, in the cruel lands to the south.

Brain kept saying go away from the bank, but heart counseled to keep near my own people. So, despite the warning that brain kept repeating, I crept on my belly, as the snake glides from bush to shrub. After many minutes I heard voices above the roar of the rapids, and as I crawled nearer I was able to part the bushes and look down, maybe, ten feet. There was another small half moon of a sandy beach and, huddled together and helpless, were a group of my people. It was not good to count ten and then seven of them.

As the squirrel looks out of his hole, so I peeped and made out Joseph Theondechoren and Charles Tsondatsaa, who is my father's squaw's brother, Paul Ononhoraton, the old man Ondonterraon, the squaw Theresa, and five others who came from my village of Teanaustayae. The white brave Goupil was lying bound and by him stretched Eustace, my father. On guard with arquebus and tomahawk and knife were more than twice ten greased Iroquois.

They had not begun to torture any captives yet, so I knew there were more of our cruel enemies in the woods behind me, searching for the rest of our party. Again brain counseled to go away swiftly, and I would have heeded brain this time, but just then I heard the voice of Blackrobe, hailing the Iroquois guard, and heart said wait.

Again he hailed from a little ways up in the woods and I saw three arquebuses and many bows raised. I knew that death was pointed at my other father, but what could I, a boy, do?

One of the guards went forward and, in my eagerness to see all,

I put up my head above the reeds like a foolish snake and I deserved to be discovered as one, had not the Squaw in Blue put her robe between me and our enemies' eyes.

They did not see me, for all were watching Blackrobe, who had advanced out into the clearing and was coming steadily towards the captives' circle.

When but a spear's thrust from the first Iroquois, my other father spoke aloud: "Know, Mohawks, I carry no arquebus nor have I ever made it thunder, for that is not my way. I am the fellow traveler of these Hurons you have bound here and it is proper that I share their captivity."

At this the guard Iroquois stepped back and I saw their mind quite clearly. They feared some ambush, but I could have told them there could not be any Hurons behind my other father, for of our fighting men not five were missing from the bound captives. I felt these had gone to God.

Then Blackrobe advanced bravely, though the forward guards held their knives with threatening gestures and I feared most unhappily that they might then and there thrust them home.

But the Mohawks seemed to think otherwise. They lowered their weapons as Blackrobe kept advancing onto the open beach. When he came up with empty hands, the tall guards took my other father by the arms so that he was helpless and led him into the midst of our captives.

Seeing this, though the sun still shone down hotly on the scene, I felt black night in my heart.

Blackrobe went straight to René Goupil, and the white brave struggled up to his knees and poured forth rapid words in the language of my other father's country across the Great Lake. The Iroquois watched curiously. They are poor pagans and knew not what Goupil did, but I knew he was confessing his sins. When I saw my other father's hand make the Sign of Absolution, I touched my forehead, shoulders, and breast likewise.

There were war cries of the Iroquois from down stream and into sight came four of our enemies and they urged before their clubs a bleeding naked captive. At first I did not know him. But with the sunlight fully upon him I made him out. It was the burly William Couture and he was not nice to look upon.

Iroquois leapt upon this white brave and they screamed,, not he, as they struggled like fighting wolves on the sands. When they fell back Blackrobe went up and took Couture in his arms and then I noticed that a broken spear point was transfixing the palm of his right hand. It made me think of the wounded Hand of Jesus that day He died.

When my other father had drawn this spear point out I saw Couture's fingers and they were all like wild red roses. . . .

I had in mind to back into the woods and away from these sad sights, and the worse sights that I knew would be sure to come, but I lingered too long.

Something leapt heavily on my bare back and long fingers dug themselves deep in my neck, so that my face was buried in the pebbles and the earth. My breathing stopped and many colored lights swam before me.

Then I was plucked from the ground and flung into a thorny bush. It is not good to land in such a bush. I, Tarcisius Tandihetsi, say so.

When I had dug the earth from my eyes I saw before me an iron ankle bracelet on the bare foot of my captor, and as I looked I knew whose prisoner I was. From the left foot of him who stood over me, there was a toe not there, and the missing toe was next to the little toe.

In my Huron language Snake Tooth addressed me:

"We have the dogs and now we get the puppy who keeps watch. Get up."

I folded my arms and looked him in the face as well as I could, for the cut over my eye had reopened and it blinded me much. But

I would not let him see I was in pain. It is not right to give an apostate such pleasure.

So I told him: "I would prefer that it had been a real Iroquois who had taken me. At least they are pagans and have not received Saving Waters on their forehead and then acted sinfully as if they had not."

This I said to Snake Tooth.

He smiled evilly: "Soon the puppy will taste the bitter food that real Iroquois give captives."

I let him see that he had captured a Huron and the son of a chief. I was not afraid, even when he bound my arms with tight thongs.

Snake Tooth drove me before him out of the forest and down to the sandy beach. I went gladly for I knew it was better to be reunited with Eustace and my other father than to wander unarmed in the wilds by the Great River where, when black night came, a lynx or a wolf could spring on me.

When I had been driven within an arrow's flight of my people I saw Blackrobe kneeling by William Couture and trying to help him, for he bled most freely from many places. Snake Tooth saw these two talking together and the Iroquois guards standing by and watching them. Snake Tooth did not like to see them speak with each other. He prodded me sharply with the deer's horn in the end of his war club so that I leapt up like a startled mallard.

Then he flung me to a Mohawk guard and strode up to two tall young braves who wore red-stained headpieces.

With angry words Snake Tooth shouted so that all the Iroquois could hear: "You have no sense. Do you not see that the white men are talking together in their vile language and Ondesonk is congratulating this bleeding dog because he killed Two Beavers? And you, Two Beavers' sons, look on."

I remembered the other tall Iroquois chief I had seen fall before Couture's arquebus in the fight by the edge of the reeds. But

I knew that Snake Tooth spoke with a slit tongue, for my other father was only consoling the white brave.

But the false words of Snake Tooth were believed and, as I watched, helpless, other Iroquois warriors with fists and war clubs and the yells of the demons fell upon Blackrobe. Quickly they bore him to the ground. He did not resist. They tore his worn robe away and left him only his shirt and the sting of many cruel blows.

He lay face down on the sands and I thought they had killed my other father, but I remembered bitterly our enemies do not so with important captives. It is not their way. And fear came to my heart when I remembered their custom of red gauntlets and slow fires.

These enemies were leaving my other father, when the two young braves whom Snake Tooth had called Two Beavers' sons, leapt upon his body like a wounded bear attacks. Each grabbed one of Blackrobe's limp hands and raised them to their teeth. . . .

It is very painful to have your nails torn out, and my other father moaned so that I heard him and so did the other captives. But what could we do? Our turn would come later in the castles of the enemy.

I heard the squaw Theresa weeping, for she also liked Blackrobe. Though my heart was heavy I did not weep. I am Tarcisius, a chief's son.

Then the sons of the slain Two Beavers threw my other father over so that his face, all twisted in agony, was in the sunshine and, like the village dogs that they were, they crunched Blackrobe's forefingers till I, lying the space of three canoes away, heard the bones crack.

With this they flung down my other father's hands and when they went away he attempted to rise, but the strength was not in him and he sank back. And when I looked at him again, his two nice hands were not nice any longer but, like Couture's, they were as wild red rose buds. . . .

Chapter Five

Booty and the Beasts

IT IS HARD when you want to help and cannot do so, and that was the way I, Tarcisius Tandihetsi, felt now. For I tried to go to my other father, and an Iroquois with a coiled snake tattooed on his breast, whom I was to know as Birch Bark, stopped my crawling forward by knocking me sharply on the head with his war club.

All went starry, then black. When my head did clear, and the river, sky, and the green banks stopped going round and round about me, I saw Iroquois coming in burdened with the canvas bags that held the Mission supplies. I knew these contained many sacred things that the Blackrobes used and I felt sorry that these painted pagans should handle them.

The apostate Huron, Snake Tooth, was the captain of this war party. He gave harsh orders and Iroquois sprang into the reeds upstream and floated out their hidden canoes. Other Iroquois bent down saplings and took out their paddles which had been so skillfully concealed in the branches that I had looked at the saplings and seen only the leaves.

Our captors had twelve canoes hidden in the reeds and five of our canoes would still ride on the water.

Into these were heaped all the packages of booty and then they clubbed the wounded down to the water's edge, if they did not run fast enough.

The canoe I was flung into contained also my father, Eustace.

29

He was bound and bleeding in many places, but you could see he was still a captain and there was no fear in his eyes as he looked straight at his enemies. I tried to be like him, for I am a chief's son.

It was easy to see that the Iroquois did not wish to stay in this place of our ambushing. They dreaded some strong party of French traders with arquebuses might come paddling along. It is safer for them to fight with us Hurons, who are armed mostly with bow and club.

The Iroquois, Birch Bark, was towing the canoe I lay in. I could not help thinking of an hour ago when my other father had his nice hands on the gunwale. That made me think of Blackrobe's hands now, as I had seen them on the sandy beach of our capture. My thoughts were not pleasant and I did not let myself think of the things that were ahead of us. For often I have heard my people say the Iroquois will subject you to an hundred deaths before death itself ensues. The Iroquois are more than pagans, they are savage wolves.

We got through the rapids, and Birch Bark and another Iroquois who wore a necklace of bears' claws, came into our canoe and began paddling. I must have fallen asleep, for next I remember muttering a drowsy prayer to the Squaw in Blue as my other father had taught me. Then I forgot my prayer, for I was being kicked into full wakefulness.

We were no longer in the Great River, but had turned into the mouth of the narrower River of the Iroquois. Ahead of us was another long beach below a thick fringe of spruce and on it painted Iroquois with many shouts that were not pleasant were herding the captives.

Birch Bark cut my thongs and, robbing me of my anklet and bracelets, made me carry bundles of our Mission supplies to a place beyond the waterline, where Snake Tooth and the other Iroquois captains were dividing the booty.

I made seven trips to the spot where our enemies were ripping open all the bundles.

They are dogs, these Iroquois. And it was not pleasant for a Christian to see these savages paw over the embroidered vestments and sacred vessels intended for the beautiful birch-bark chapel in our village.

I saw some of our captors put over their painted skins the vestments that the Blackrobes wear when they say the Mass.

Right before me by the canoe side Birch Bark pulled out of a ripped-open Mission bag the golden and white Mass gown that the virgin girls had made with their needles in their long convent at Quebec. I knew this was a gift for my other father from the squaw in charge of the virgin girls.

Another Iroquois brave saw this prize and wanted this gown. He sprang forward. Both started to pull it as village dogs do sometimes with a stolen bear's bone. It did not come in two pieces as I expected it would. Angry words these braves screamed. Pulling hard, both reached for their knives and while I watched they tugged and slashed at each other. Once they fought so close to me that I heard them panting. I fell back beyond the reach of the flashing knives into the river. When I got up Birch Bark had missed a thrust and his knife slashed a long tear in the gold embroidered cross on the Mass gown. This angered more the other brave. I saw cunning creep into his eyes. He made believe to tug hard at his end of the Mass gown, but he let go and Birch Bark fell backwards with the gown. As an eagle swoops, the Iroquois landed upon Birch Bark, one grasping hand at his throat, and with his knife he sought for his enemy's heart below the coiled snake tattooed there.

I felt glad in my own heart that one of our captors would fall into the flames that do not go out. But as the point of his blade touched Birch Bark's breast, I saw this Iroquois brave rise up and then sink to one side on the golden and white Mass gown. Just the hilt of Birch Bark's knife showed in his side.

Then I felt gladder for I remembered this Iroquois dog was one I had seen tearing out my other father's nails.

Birch Bark kicked the knife from the limp hand and it fell into the running water. He leaned over and took the three fresh Huron scalp locks that hung to the apron. He fastened them at his own side. Then he dragged the body to the water and let it float away on the current.

He poked his head through the slash in the stained golden and white Mass gown and gathering the trailing ends of it around his shoulder, like an elk robe, drove me ahead of him till we rounded the bushes on the point and joined the howling mob of Iroquois who were now dancing about the huddled captives.

All the Mission packages were cut open and scattered everywhere. One whooping Mohawk Iroquois had thrust his head through a picture of Saint Ignatius and wore it around his neck like a collar. His three eagle feathers bobbed and waved as he leapt and yelled. The torn edges of the picture flapped too.

Another young brave with a reliquary dangling from his neck had a small bell that the altar boy rings at Mass. He shook this wildly and once he came close and struck me with it on the shoulder. It was as bad as a war-club blow.

Many of the Iroquois had lighted white wax candles and yellow tapers that they had looted from the Mission bags. They were thrusting these at the helpless captives.

When some of these dancing demons saw me standing beyond the circle, they held these lights out to my bare sides. Burning candles are better than war clubs to make you move faster. I dove between the dancing lines, stumbled over a torn Missal that some Mohawk had abandoned, and found I had landed beside my father, Eustace, and the old man, Ondonterraon. Both were bound so that they could not defend themselves. . . .

It was good that Birch Bark had forgotten to rebind my arms with deer thongs. For the candles had lighted pains on my sides. When Eustace saw that I did not moan, he comforted: "Courage,

Tarcisius." He would have said more, but an Iroquois kicked him in the face, which is a very great insult to a captain. I forgot my paining sides when I saw this. But I remembered likewise how easily Birch Bark had slain his fellow Iroquois. Captives are more helpless.

The old man Ondonterraon called me with his eyes and I turned to lie nearer to him.

"Little Spoon," he said, "remember that I am very old and I feel that I will not travel much more. Find Ondesonk and tell him I desire Saving Waters before the long journey."

Ondonterraon was still a pagan, and I nodded.

Here Snake Tooth cried an order and our tormentors ceased their dance.

I looked up. Blackrobe was on the other side of the group of captives, near Goupil. I saw he was giving Absolution to Hurons who lay bound near him.

Now the majority of the enemy trooped to the spruce trees that were above the beach, and some braves began to paint on trees peeled of their bark the red-colored record of their expedition's success. This is an Iroquois custom. I hoped some fellow Hurons would see these markings and carry word to my village and my father's squaw, Catherine.

About these braves grouped many Iroquois who wore the Mission Mass gowns, black and green and red; and I saw Birch Bark's golden and white booty with its drying brown stain.

I watched sorrowfully till our guards unloosened the foot bonds of my people and drove us down to the water's edge.

This was my chance and I wormed myself to the side of my other father. With haste I told him the old man Ondonterraon's wish for Saving Waters.

While I spoke I could not take my eyes from Blackrobe's finger tips. Cruel they were and what my own pains had not made my eyes do, this sight of his hands that would not be nice any more, made them do.

But now he had no time for my tears. He left me and hobbled to Ondonterraon. Stooping at the water's surface, he shelled his wounded right hand and I saw Saving Waters fall on the bent forehead of Ondonterraon. The old man's face lighted and its wrinkles seemed to smooth out. He looked like a brave in his prime. He did not look his fourscore of years any longer.

The guards were dividing the captives into the various canoes for the long journey into their country. I tried to be put in the canoe with Eustace and my other father, but Birch Bark called out that I was his—I and the old man, Ondonterraon.

He strode down and pushed the old man towards his canoe. But Ondonterraon stood ground and, folding his arms and looking his enemy in the eye, cried so that all might hear him:

"Mohawk master, at my age one does not care to visit foreign countries, and one cannot adapt himself to new ways of life. If you wish to put me to death, why not do so now?"

I knew that these bold words to Birch Bark, whom I had seen slay one of his own people only a few minutes before, were as a flame to leaves in deer-time.

The Mohawk reached back for his tomahawk. He took a short run, as the boys in my village do when we play leaping games. Still in the air, I saw the hatchet whirl and its edge bury itself in the skull of the old man Ondonterraon. Like a sack of yellow corn that had been ripped the old man's body collapsed. His head struck the gunwale of Birch Bark's canoe, but the tomahawk did not fly out.

Then Ondonterraon rolled over and lay face down in the water. And Birch Bark had to lift the dripping head to get the scalp lock. But I knew the old man Ondonterraon had gone to God ahead of us captives with Saving Waters still damp on his forehead. I felt glad within my heart.

At Birch Bark's grunted order I climbed into his canoe. Silently my Iroquois captor bound my arms and my legs to the bottom of his canoe till I lay as helpless as a bundle of Mission goods. He threw the stained Mass gown over me. Through the slit I saw him and another Iroquois get in. We started for the country of our southern enemies.

I had much to think about, and my thoughts were not pleasant. I, Tarcisius Tandihetsi, say so.

Chapter Six

Locked Antlers

IT WAS FIVE dreadful days later that my thongs were cut again and this is how it came about. After ascending the River of the Iroquois and embarking on the long narrow Lake Patawabouque (Lake Champlain) with its succession of pine-crowded islands and wild wooded points we had come into early afternoon.

My people I had seen only across the evening campfires, when we were stretched helpless on the ground and braves would amuse themselves by irritating with their long sharp nails our festering wounds. Never was I able to speak with my other father but once when at gray dawn Blackrobe was led near where I lay. He smiled down and blessed me with his mangled hands. For many hours I remembered that.

By daylight Birch Bark and his Iroquois companion, Partridge, whom I disliked very much, were hunters and scouts. They paddled ahead of the main fleet. When they went ashore I was left bound in the canoe. Nearly always they returned empty handed and what little food there was the Iroquois saved and ate. Our share was a few berries.

So this early afternoon there was a gnawing in my belly like a gray wolf—two gray wolves, it was more like.

Partridge was bow paddle. It amused him whenever he thought of it, to turn back and say politely: "The sun streams too hotly on my young nephew. Let me cool his sides." And then with his dripping paddle he would make on my blistered sides the Sign he had seen us Christian Hurons make when we blessed ourselves.

This was very painful, but I would try not to show Partridge that I felt it. I am Tarcisius Tandihetsi and a chief's son.

Again he had scraped where those candles had burnt me. I looked at him as bad as I could with my good eye, for the other was still swollen from the wound I had received at the beginning of our taking.

He grinned and he called back to Birch Bark: "Our Huron puppy would like to bite.

"Why don't you growl?" And he hit me sharply over the head. "Lie still, then, puppy," he bullied.

The blow threw me on my side and I stayed that way where it was not necessary to watch the naked, greased back of my tormentor.

Lying there on my side and feeling very miserable about everything, I could watch the towering rocks on the silent shore we were paddling near. The canoe came close under a lonely point. There in a crack in the side of the sheer brownish rock was a sturdy young cedar.

I watched it growing all alone in that rocky wall till the gunwale of the canoe hid it from me and a thought came to me that made me feel stronger.

He Who makes all things put that cedar there and gave it soil to grow and did not let it die. Neither will He desert me, for I know what Blackrobe has so often told me, that I am dearer to Him than many trees.

Then I tried not to think of my empty belly but it was very hard. I would keep repeating: "Jesus, have pity on us and send us something to eat. Jesus, have pity on us."

And I could not help thinking of our Huron villages many leagues to the north, where in the long lodges were smoked fish and eels, maize, and bear's meat in the kettles.

The memory of my father's squaw came up and I saw Catherine wearing her beaver robe, ornamented at the edges with mooseskin, and her collar of porcelain beads with the medal of the Squaw in Blue on her breast. I felt more than hungry then for I realized that Catherine and my village, with every stroke of Birch Bark's and Partridge's paddles, were growing farther away and the terrible country of our captors with the Iroquois fires awaiting us, coming ever closer.

Always I would find my thoughts coming back to the chase and the desire of food. Berries do not fill your belly. And I would again repeat: "Jesus, Who owns the animals, have pity on us."

I was saying this to myself, like answering a litany, when I saw what made my thongs be cut and filled my belly.

We had come close in to a sloping bank. The pines grew down in thousands. Birch Bark and Partridge were silently paddling. Their eyes were looking ahead. And they would have passed by had I not called out to them.

For in the half shadows below a towering pine something struggled and half of it seemed to sink down. I thought the fever was on me once again. But I shook it off and kept looking at the pines.

I wished very much that I had the long wonder-stick that a Blackrobe at the Great Village on the Rock let me look through. We Hurons called it Makes Far Away Come Near. It is not magic. This I know, for my other father looked through it, and he does not use sorcerer's magic. If I had Makes Far Away Come Near now I could easily have seen what was under that great pine.

Then I was sure there was something living there and I called to Birch Bark: "Iroquois, look there below the tall pine, where the bushes are thick. Something strange struggles."

Both Iroquois ceased paddling and Birch Bark's hand was on his weapon. But they saw nothing for it was still in the bushes now. I told him most earnestly what I had observed.

Partridge was about to scrape me again with his cruel paddle, but Birch Bark had caught sight of a movement. At his command

Partridge turned the canoe's bow and we went swiftly toward the still bank.

I craned my neck and in the half shadows of the pines there was a sharp rustling and now the brown quarters of an animal tried to rise.

Partridge whipped up his bow and sped an arrow into the half shadows. Birch Bark called out: "It's a buck."

On the instant our canoe scraped the bottom, the two Iroquois leapt, hatchets in hand. I saw them disappear into the shadows below the pines.

I knew by their cries that they had come upon meat. It made me very hungry. I asked the Squaw in Blue to make these hunters have soft hearts towards me.

Birch Bark silently appeared over the gunwale. He grabbed my nose and he held his reddened tomahawk menacingly over my face, till I thought my time to go to God was here.

I felt suddenly glad and I looked at him steadily.

His eagle feathers brushed my cheek as he swept the tomahawk down to where my feet were tied and he cut my leg thongs.

"Come ashore," he ordered. "The Huron puppy has keen sight. He has filled our bellies."

He lifted me as though I were a bag of Mission supplies and threw me on the sandy shore.

At first, I was not able to walk. But when I was there in the half shadows, I saw what I had discovered.

Two spotted bucks had locked antlers in a fight not many days before and they had struggled their strength away trying to unlock their horns. Now they lay, gaunt, their ribs commencing to show and one was kicking his last.

As I looked on the fresh meat, the buck's kickings ceased.

The two Mohawk Iroquois took a quarter of one animal and then they arranged a signal over the slaughtered beasts that the main party could see.

We paddled ahead and at that night's camp I ate my share of broiled steaks.

Before we started ahead next morning I learnt that only my arms were to be kept bound hereafter.

Birch Bark warned me: "If our puppy should attempt to run away from his kind keepers, this is what I shall do to him."

With that he lifted me so that I lay helpless in his strong arms and held the soles of my feet to the embers of our campfire. Before they burnt he drew me back. But I knew that he meant it.

We pushed on ahead of the fleet. I was to learn that my captors were not only savages but pagans.

Chapter Seven

The Invisible People

WE KEPT PADDLING ahead of the main party and shortly after the sun was up over the eastern shore of the lake Partridge sighted several specks in the distance.

"They are Iroquois canoes," claimed Birch Bark, but Partridge was not so certain. At once we drifted and my two captors held a consultation out there on the lake where we were half a league from any shore. Birch Bark's opinion prevailed, that the canoes ahead were friends. When we had paddled closer, signals were exchanged.

Eight Iroquois in their red and blue barred paint, greased and stripped for the warpath, were in the canoes. Their cruel cries were those of delight, when Birch Bark told them of his party coming on behind and the twenty-three captives. These scouts told us that on an island less than half a day's paddling were encamped more than two hundred Mohawks going on the warpath to the Great River.

Not more than four hours later we came in sight of this main war party. They must have paddled thirty canoes. I had never seen so many together, even at the Great Village on the Rock. We passed through the midst of these paddling braves, but did not stop.

It did not make me feel good to hear Partridge taunt me: "Huron puppy, your brothers and the white braves will entertain that fleet when they camp this evening. It is too bad the puppy will miss the welcome." He poked me with his oar. I do not like Partridge and I did a foolish thing.

41

My feet were free of thongs, since I had discovered the two bucks yesterday, and I kicked out sharply at my tormentor. My heel caught him in the stomach and the canoe almost upset as he started back. His paddle flew overboard.

Before I could kick again, the long nails of Birch Bark were buried in my bare shoulders. With the thongs about my arms I was helpless to defend myself and Partridge, grabbing me by the ankles, mocked me saying: "Our little brother is too warm. Let me cool him."

He tossed me over the gunwale. Though I struggled like an eel I could not for long keep my lips above surface. With his thumbs pressing my toes, Partridge held my ankles and kept bending them upward, driving my face below. I choked and smothered.

I do not now remember how long I was unconscious. I do not remember my captors lifting me back into the canoe. But when consciousness came back to me, my toes were aching and I was no longer even wet. The stars were out and both Iroquois were paddling silently and steadily over the smooth waters. It was long after their usual camping time.

When they did stop for the night's encampment, my toes were still aching in agony and I must have been lying there awake till the stars went out of the skies.

Once I recalled wishfully what my other father had said so gayly that last night we camped together before our ambush: "Tarcisius, we sleep at the Sign of the Beautiful Star. For we who have God with us, rest calmly anywhere."

Then I tried to ask the Squaw in Blue to make the pains go away and finally I slept.

In the day's light I saw we had stopped at a flinty beach. This place Birch Bark called Point Ticonderoga and I learnt the Iroquois warriors always stopped here going and returning from their raids along the Great River.

My thongs were cut and when I was able to use my arms I spent the rest of the long hot day heaping up piles of flints. I was kept at this work till weak from hunger. Neither Mohawk had given me any food since yesterday when they killed the spotted deers with the locked antlers. I plucked strawberries but they did not fill the belly.

When I asked Partridge for food, he smiled: "It is not good to give puppies too much on the trail. Go down to the shore and lap up some water."

I did this, and there I saw the canoes of our main party coming.

I stood by the piles of flints I had gathered when each canoe came in and beached. Horror of what was ahead came into my heart as I saw the torn and bleeding people being driven ashore. I looked for those I loved and the thought came, maybe, these demons had killed them last night.

Then two canoes were beached. The two poor white braves were in one, but my eyes were on the other canoe. In it with Snake Tooth was Eustace, my father. I forgot all about the other captives. He was raw as fresh meat. . . .

I ran forward, and then I saw my father's two thumbs were gone and his arms were swollen as fat muskrats.

I tried to get to him, but that son of the slain Two Beavers, they called Curly Dog, hurled me away with his club. Half stunned I was rising to one knee, for the flinty beach cut deep, when two streaming hands tried to lift me gently and I was gazing up into the streaked and blackened face of my other father.

"Little Tarcisius, so here you are. I looked and looked and hoped you had escaped."

Hastily I told my Blackrobe I was Birch Bark's captive. Then I listened while Blackrobe told me the captives had been made to run the gauntlet when they met the two hundred Mohawk Iroquois last night, and he concluded: "I am glad my Tarcisius was not there."

Here Partridge yelled at me and my other father told me to go promptly.

"In all that you can, obey them," he said, "and the Good God Who sees will strengthen and reward Tarcisius."

All next day we captives were busy gathering flints and I learnt that this Point Ticonderoga was a place of wicked superstitions.

Toward evening the piles of flints were high enough and we were herded together. The guards did not bind us, for now we were far into the enemy's country. And many of the captives were not even able to gather flints. I managed to wiggle through my people till I stood between the white brave, René Goupil, and my other father.

Standing there we watched the Iroquois. Their tattooed sorcerers had put on wolf-head masks. Then they took up tortoise shells, half full of pebbles, and striking them against their masks and chanting to their devils, they began a leaping dance. It was not like any I had seen our Huron pagans dance and I said to my Blackrobe:

"Are they going to burn us now?"

"No; those who will go to God through the fires of the Iroquois will be in the villages to the south. This is pagan practice. Snake Tooth told me."

"My ears are itching, other father."

Blackrobe laid torn hands on my shoulders while he spoke: "It seems our pagan captors believe that in the waters off this Point Ticonderoga there dwell a tribe of invisible people whose favor they must gain."

"If they are invisible, how do the Iroquois know they are there?" This I asked my Blackrobe.

"Tarcisius must know that this is silly nonsense. It is our dear Lord of the Waves Who causes the winds to blow that ruffle the surface of the lake at this point. There are no such things as water spirits. But these poor pagans are easily led to believe what the Father of Lies wishes them. So they hold these invisible people make the flints and scatter them along these shores."

"That is superstition. He Who makes all," I said, "makes the flints as He makes other stones. Indeed, they are pagans and cruel savages. And they all are going to burn forever."

I must have said this hotly, for my father went on:

"And so, Little Spoon, our brothers the Iroquois in their blindness believe these invisible people will send strong winds and high waves that will swamp the bark canoes, unless they make these water spirits suitable offerings."

Here the white brave, Goupil, put in: "That must be what their witch doctors are about to do."

All about us the Iroquois were shouting and singing the high notes of some chant and dancing as though they were stepping on glowing coals. I had it in my mind to wish these sands were fires, but I put that thought away quickly, lest my other father should know that I carried the Devil in my heart.

So I looked and ten sorcerers had come in a line down to the water's edge. Here they stopped and the braves opened their tobacco pouches, embroidered with porcupine quills, and offered them bits of tobacco.

Then wading into the water up to their knees, the sorcerers chanted some demon song and began throwing bits of tobacco upon the surface. Three times they came back for more tobacco.

When the Iroquois warriors had made their offerings, I saw Snake Tooth and other chiefs measuring out so much tobacco for each pile of flints we had gathered.

I felt pity in my heart, seeing Snake Tooth, who had Saving Waters on his forehead, thus doing devil practices again. Our pagan captors did not know better, but this apostate did.

When the invisible people were paid, Goupil said to Blackrobe: "Father Jogues, do you see that most of the tobacco these demons cast upon the waves is from our Mission supplies. It is the good tobacco that came from Quebec."

Blackrobe shrugged his shoulders.

45

"And can we complain if the waves get it rather than the Iroquois? Certainly the Fathers on the unfortunate Huron Mission will smoke the tobacco of the natives for another year. It is very vile tobacco."

My other father seemed to have forgotten me, for he said: "René, René, does not your heart bleed for these blinded children who know not the Giver of all good things? At least, we may propitiate Him by our sufferings and the sufferings that lie ahead."

The white brave replied: "Father, may God be blessed! May His Holy Will be done! I accept these crosses. I desire them. I embrace them with all my strength."

"These are sentiments from my own heart, my son," said Blackrobe. "We sow and others will reap. Thus it has always been, and here in the New World in these strange lands to the south whither we are driven like sheep to the slaughter, there will be no exception."

I thought Blackrobe seemed happy and yet he must have ached very much from his raw wounds. This puzzled me. But now I could not put my puzzle in words of question. It is hard to be a captive and not free.

Then the sorcerers came wading ashore. Our captors were joyous, thinking they had paid the invisible people for a successful passage south. They even fed us well on deer meat and squashes, cooked in embers.

We stretched out on the dark earth while Iroquois braves guarded us. I thought over what I had seen this day at Point Ticonderoga and the thought that came most vividly into my mind was that the enemy were feeding us, not because they wanted us to live, but because they did not want us to die of exhaustion before we came into their villages to the south. I turned over to ask my other father, but he was already sleeping soundly, as though he was back in the Blackrobes' long lodge of my village of Teanaustayae.

I searched and clasped his poor hand, no longer a nice hand, but all swollen and festered, and I pressed my lips to it. He groaned in his sleep. He did not wake. But I felt better, just holding that hand, for I remembered it was the hand that had touched God. And pleasant thoughts came, clear as stars in the Great Bear above, that real invisible people watched us—our angels, the Squaw in Blue, and He Who makes all.

Then I too fell into a sleep without dreams.

Chapter Eight

The Welcome of the Mohawks

I LEARNT in the following days why the captives' bonds were cut away and they were fed. For we soon came to the shore called Where the Lake Closes (Lake George). Here the canoes were drawn up and hidden. Again the paddles were fastened artfully in the upper branches of saplings, so that even I, Tarcisius Tandihetsi, could not see them an arrow's flight away.

The march across country began. My people were the beasts of burden. On our livid shoulders were put the Mission bags from our plundered canoes. We were driven, weary league after league, along the narrow Mohawk trail. Always we went single file, so our footprints would be destroyed. This is the custom, lest a hostile war party from the Cat Nation would come across our trail and learn our numbers.

The afternoon of this day I carried my share and walked through strange thick woods before Blackrobe. We came to a stream Birch Bark called Oiogue, which means Beautiful River. The ford was deep and we Christian Hurons had to swim the space of many paces with our packs. Blackrobe swims, and I swim, of course, but some of the captives who could not almost drowned.

We were driven on faster now with sharp sticks and I thought we were never to stop and rest. Before I could say my thoughts out loud to my other father, we were halted.

I saw Snake Tooth and other captains take up large conch shells that were by the trail side and blow into them. Soon other conch shells were blown ahead. Then more.

Birch Bark, at my shoulder, answered my question: "That is to tell our village of Ossernenon we are returning with many captives and bags of plunder, Huron puppy. They will hear and prepare the welcome that is fitting.

"Even now—listen—that means the squaws are hurrying to the landing place from the corn fields."

He grinned as the Devil must and I edged away, for I had learnt when he looked that way his heart was crueler.

Blackrobe whispered to me: "Courage, my little one, and be thankful to Our Saviour, for the joys of Heaven are purchased only by partaking of His sufferings."

He then told me this was the Eve of the Assumption, and he added: "I have thought, Tarcisius, that this day of so much rejoicing in Heaven will prove unto us a day of keen sufferings."

As we came out into the clearing, there was a wide peaceful river below us. More conch shells sounded faintly from the other green shore.

On the crest of this hill opposite stood the wooden palisades of a large village of two hundred fires. More than a score of the bark-roofed long lodges showed above the thick triple rows of the palisades.

I heard Blackrobe saying to Paul Ononhoraton:

"This is the castle of my brothers, the Mohawks, that I have desired these many months to see." His face did not look sad as he gazed across the broad valley.

With stinging blows our captors hustled us down trail to the riverside and piled us with the bags of plunder into the canoes. When we were driven out on the village shore our guards began stripping us bare as stripling poles in their palisades. Birch Bark would not even let me wear the medal of the Squaw in Blue that my Blackrobe gave me long ago, though I begged him this many times. I, Tarcisius Tandihetsi, do not like to beg. He kept grinning. He told me to look up.

There swarming down the hillside came more than four hundred howling Iroquois; old braves and skin-gowned squaws with porcelain collars and ear pendants and whooping children. What took my eyes and made fear come into my heart, though I did not wish to show it, was the sight of all armed with thorny sticks and rods of iron.

An old captive Algonquin hobbled forward. He was carrying a freshly killed deer on his back. He spoke to Blackrobe and René Goupil. His words were: "White men, you are lost. There is no hope for you. Prepare to die. The stakes are ready. You will be burnt."

I had not time to think over what he had said, for in the midst of my twenty-two companions I was prodded forward. About us swarmed the howling Iroquois. Many of the boys and girls who were about my height swished their thorny sticks and pointed at me. But I did not show any fear in my face. Of this I am sure. It would not be right, for I am Tarcisius Tandihetsi, a chief's son. I did say under my breath: "Jesus have pity on me and make me strong and silent like Eustace and my other father." This I repeated many times.

Now a village captain with a necklace of keys, plundered from some white settlement, made the shrieking crowd of our enemies stop and when it was all still there in the hot afternoon, he spoke mockingly to us: "My brothers, Sun has given you into our hands. We thank Sun. You have come down the lakes and through the forests to our country. You have carried your presents on your backs. You must be weary of the trail. Your shoulders are red from the burdens. I see among our brothers, the Hurons, three white men. They also have come. We thank Sun. A welcome is prepared for each. For you are our brothers and you must be tired from your long journey. So, courage, my brothers."

Here this Iroquois captain grinned at me, for I was the only small one among the captives, and pointed me out to the boys and girls.

Birch Bark whispered in my ear: "See, Huron puppy, Kicking Bear urges our children of your own height to bid you welcome. They are eager."

I saw well enough how anxious they were, as they whirled their thorny sticks and like slender demons yelled insulting things at me. But I know that my thoughts did not show in my face.

Our guards were lining us up and I saw them place William Couture first, because he had killed one of their chiefs, Two Beavers. Eustace, my father, was stationed near the center. Behind him René Goupil came, and Paul and Bernard and Theresa. Last in the line was placed Blackrobe.

I was left standing alone and I began to hope that I would not be made to run the gauntlet, when that apostate Snake Tooth called out mockingly: "Little Spoon, we wish to make you happy too. Ondesonk has taught you Christians the more you suffer on earth, the happier you will be in Heaven.

"These children will make your Heaven happier,"—he pointed with his stick to the young ones of the village, who grinned broadly—"because they already love you and you ought to thank them."

I did not feel like thanking them, for I knew in my heart these young Mohawks with their sticks would be more savage than the braves or squaws. But I put a mask of calmness on my face and did not show them what was in my heart. It is the best way.

Here the Iroquois chief. Kicking Bear, cried out in his loud voice: "Listen, children, I put our little nephew before the white sorcerer, Ondesonk. This is my order. Welcome the Huron puppy to our village, but remember this, my children, he is young. His sides are tender. No iron rods are to be used on them. This is my order."

"Come, Wild Berries," he addressed a boy my height, "see the puppy does not run, lest he lose breath."

Wild Berries grinned and stationed himself directly in the line before me.

It was very hard to grin back in his face, but I did it.

It was still as a dark night in the forest as we stood there in the glaring sun and the twin lines of Mohawks before us were as intent as so many lynx about to spring down on a fallow deer.

Blackrobe put his hand on my shoulder and spoke softly: "Strong heart and courage, Tarcisius mine. We stand on the narrow path to Heaven. Say 'Jesus,' 'Mary' and strength to go up the hill will be given to you."

Then somewhere a conch shell blew and all the Mohawks began the low chant of the Torture Dance. As they formed and circled, ever moving faster, their voices rose to a frenzy. It was the hooting of demons.

I kept saying "Jesus, Mary" as I heard my other father doing.

Finally, the two yelling lines closed in like waves rushing together in a storm; only a narrow lane was left open between them, leading to the stage on the crest of the hill.

Another conch shell blew. Flint-pointed spears prodded the first of the captives toward the lane, and the chain commenced to climb the steep hill. The welcome of Ossernenon had begun. . . .

Stinging pain drove me forward in my turn. I soon found the braves and squaws lashed their sticks at me, but did not touch me heavily. The boys and girls along the bloody lane were more cruel.

"Puppy. Puppy. Huron puppy," they kept chanting.

I staggered on in a whirlpool of blows and kicks that stung and stung until I could have shrieked, but, remembering Blackrobe, I kept repeating the Holy Name and the name of the Squaw in Blue.

I could not run, for this Wild Berries before me checked my speed by hitting me across the face with the bracelet on his wrist.

Once he was hit himself with a blow intended for me and he did not like it.

Soon the hillside became as slippery as though it had been raining. Through pools of bright red I slipped and when I fell, boys and girls would pinch and lash me till Wild Berries jerked me to my feet.

"Puppy. Puppy. Huron puppy." I began to hear it as though from across the wide River of the Mohawks. My body felt one stinging sore and I had to wipe my eyes to see the sunshine.

It seemed that I could bear no more. I would never reach the stage on the crest of that awfully long hillside. In spite of my will I groaned aloud. Thorny sticks stung me to my feet again.

Then Birch Bark appeared and drove some of the boys and girls and their maddening sticks away from me.

I staggered on after the slippery line. At the foot of the stage I slipped and did not try to get up.

Birch Bark carried at the end of a sling an iron ball that must have weighed two pounds. This he swung over his head and shouted to the boys and girls who were still tormenting me. They gave back unwillingly. He kicked me forward and again I fell. Here the ground was damp, as if a little crimson brook flowed by, and all the grass was flecked.

As I got to my feet, for the first time I saw my other father. I would not have known him. I had forgotten he was the captive behind me. My Blackrobe was horribly lacerated from the nails and thorns on the Iroquois sticks. As I looked at him in pity, Birch Bark swung his iron ball and let it go at Blackrobe. It caught him in the middle of his streaming back and down he went like a limb torn from a tree in a gale. His mangled hands shot out before his head and almost touched me. He did not make any movements. Prone he lay. Like demons on the damned, Birch Bark and other Iroquois braves leapt at him with their nail-studded clubs. . . .

They beat him back into consciousness. As he rose I saw his face. Not a spot of white was in it, except about his eyes.

I heard him muttering thickly: "Jesus. Jesus. All for Thee."

These words I repeated as Wild Berries pushed me roughly onto the stage.

Here in all positions my people lay and twisted. They did not need the thongs of deer skin, for none of them was able to crawl down.

It was very slippery on the surface of the stage, the deer flies were everywhere, and the sun was very hot. . . .

And later, a voice that I did not recognize murmured in my ear: "Puppy. Brave puppy of Christ."

I turned my aching head and saw the words came from the swollen lips of my Blackrobe. Despite my pains I felt happy within my breast. It was like my other father to think of me and say soothing words in his own greater agony.

Chapter Nine

The Mercy of the Children

WE HAD NOT been lying long on this stage outside the village palisades when squaws, with their black hair parted and tied behind with bright red-painted eel skins, came with earthenware jars and gave each of us cooling drinks. One of these was Jane, an Algonquin Christian squaw. She gave me two drinks. Coming to Blackrobe, she murmured soft words of pity and tried to stop some of his wounds, but a young boy brandished a war club that was too heavy for him and drove her off. This boy I heard Partridge address as Jumping Rabbit. I did not like him and I was to like him less. He yelled many insulting and false words about the Prayer at us.

Soon our rest time was over and the apostate, Snake Tooth, sprang on the stage. He called out and the taunting and wild dancing below stopped. He had to yell out louder and hurl his stick into the midst of a group before the Iroquois boys ceased their shoutings.

Then he invited: "Young men of Ossernenon, come and caress the white braves first. Their arquebuses have thundered and broken the peace. They are traitors. They have broken their promises. For their arquebuses have thundered and Two Beavers did not return with us."

When he said these things, the son of the slain chief—I knew by this time his name was Curly Dog—leapt for the stage at the head of the young braves. They left us Hurons alone, except to walk over us, and they began to rain blows on the backs of the two white braves and my Blackrobe. Curly Dog had a club as thick around as my thigh and with this he deliberately dealt three blows on William Couture and René Goupil. When he came to my other father, he seemed to go wild with hate. It showed mostly in his eyes. He noticed that Blackrobe had as yet three nails left. Curly Dog threw down his club. He leapt on Blackrobe. . . .

Blackrobe had none when I looked again. I tried to show my pity, but the Mohawks had turned to the Huron captives. It was awful on that stage.

A voice yelled a command in my ear. "Huron puppy, come here." It was Curly Dog who spoke.

Some one kicked me forward and I crawled over to where Blackrobe lay twisting.

Curly Dog held a fragment of shell sharpened into a knife. He grabbed my right hand and holding out the thumb looked me in the eye. I looked him in the eye, but within my breast I felt he was going to saw off my right thumb. Hastily I said a prayer to his Guardian Angel and it is true that this painted Curly Dog dropped my hand.

Then he thrust this stone knife into my unwilling hand and ordered: "Hack off Ondesonk's thumb."

He held the streaming left hand of my other father towards me. Blackrobe did not recognize me, for he could hardly see with his eyes. They were bruised and livid and swollen closed. But they were not more awful than his hands that had been nice and would never be nice again.

I am Tarcisius Tandihetsi and a chief's son. So I took the stone knife and I flung it into the howling crowd. It fell slashing the naked side of Partridge, who was about to ascend the ladder steps to the stage. What he said showed he carried the Devil in his heart, but I felt better in my heart.

Then Curly Dog chewed the forefinger of my right hand till my head swam and all—the slippery stage, the howling demons below, the westering sun and the birch bark roofs of the long lodges beyond the palisades, became a whirling stream. . . .

But I would not do his bad will on my other father. Finally, this Curly Dog—and he is the captain of the dogs—took my nose between his fingers. It is the Mohawk custom to cut it off before the death blow. I thought my torturer meant to kill me then and there. And he would, had not Snake Tooth spoken words of authority and sulkily Curly Dog let me lie, twisting in my agony.

When I looked again, Jane, the Christian Algonquin squaw who had given us the cooling drinks, was being threatened with a fiery death if she did not do Curly Dog's commands.

I heard Blackrobe speak, and the trembling squaw took up the knife.

She did not know how to saw off a thumb and that made it more painful. But Blackrobe is brave as Eustace, my father. He did not utter a sound. . . .

The left thumb of my other father fell beside me. I reached to take it, for I would have stooped to kiss it there on the stage, but a mangled hand was before my lips. Blackrobe had it himself. Speaking thickly, for he was in much pain, he lifted his severed thumb on high, the way I have seen him lift the Chalice when he said the Mass in our little birch-bark chapel at Teanaustayae and I was serving him.

He said words out loud that were a prayer. Thia is what he said: "To Thee, living and true God, I present this in remembrance of the sacrifices I have offered on the altars of Thy Church——"

Here a horrible creature beyond me, that at first I did not know was William Couture, rose up like a wounded bear and began to crawl across the stage.

Blackrobe was still praying:—"as an atonement for the want of love and reverence of which I have been guilty in touching Thy Holy Body."

57

Blackrobe lowered the bloody thumb, and the white brave warned: "Do not do so, good Father Jogues, lest these savages of Iroquois see you and force you to eat that which you hold."

When Couture had said this, my other father ceased his prayer. He obeyed. He dropped the thumb. I reached for it, but before I could stop it, it slipped between the cracks in the stage.

I heard two village dogs start snarling below us. But it was better that way, for William Couture was right. These Mohawks would have made Blackrobe do what he said. Later I was to see other captives forced to do such things.

From the other side of the stage I heard some one calling out loud "Jesus. Mary. Joseph." It was René Goupil, and the squaw Theresa was being made to do to him what had been done to my other father. . . .

I too remembered those holy names and I said them under my breath. Much better then I felt. It also made me glad within my breast that, like my other father, I had not cried out before these Iroquois savages, even when that Curly Dog chewed my forefinger most painfully.

When the sun had disappeared, some wrinkled squaws, clad in greasy battered skins, were ordered to the stage and they came bringing with them shreds of Blackrobe's shirt. With these and some herbs they bandaged his hands and mine and the other tortured captives. And we were let rest.

Then Iroquois boys and girls brought us captives water and roasted ears of corn. Wild Berries gave me my share and he taunted me with what would happen in the long lodges when it was black night.

It was now growing dark overhead, but all about the stage the Mohawks carried torches that flamed up. I thought they meant to begin the slow burnings at once. It would be better that way.

When it was black night, Snake Tooth and Kicking Bear and other Iroquois captains came back and they had braves pitch all of us down from the stage. Squaws and children had to help René Goupil and Blackrobe to walk through the palisades' gate into the village.

We were divided into smaller groups and hurried away to different long lodges. I, with nine others, was taken to one of the largest lodges. There were fireplaces down the middle and many compartments either side, separated from each other by walls of skins. Papooses hung in their shallow baskets and watched us with wide eyes. Fat puppies slept curled up on mooseskin robes. Rows of dried scalp locks stretched between the lodge poles. And smoky shadows danced against the roof.

As I was led near the glowing piles of fires down the middle of the long lodge, fear came back to my heart. But no Iroquois knew it, though I saw the boys and girls of my own height watching me narrowly.

We ten stood huddled while crowds of Iroquois squatted or stood on the raised sleeping platforms that ran either side the long lodge. All were smoking their long pipes.

One by one we were staked down to the ground. The Iroquois stake down their captives the way we stake ours. That is, flat on the back with hands and feet fastened wide apart. In that position it is not easy to move and shake off the burning coals.

For the first time in many hours I stood near Eustace, my father. Except for Blackrobe, none of the captives looked more cruelly torn. That is a brave chief's misfortune. Eustace tried to smile at me, but his features twisted into a horrible grimace and he could only utter noises that did not sound like words. Then Iroquois thrust themselves between us and Eustace, my father, was staked down. Next to him was René Goupil and at the end by the lodge entrance, my Blackrobe.

I was the last one left standing and I started forward, but Birch Bark clasped my shoulder till it hurt and held me back.

"Huron puppy," he said insultingly, "lie there in the corner with the other puppies, and watch these Huron dogs squirm."

He pushed me towards the end compartment where some fat puppies slept on a mooseskin.

Jumping Rabbit and Wild Berries were told off to guard me, and Birch Bark must have forbidden them to torment me, for they did not attempt to harm my body all that night. And they drove off the other eager children who came up with hot awls and burning coals.

There in the corner I had to watch through the long black hours while the young ones of Ossernenon, as the Mohawk custom is, learnt and practiced their lessons in cruelty.

This night torture is chiefly for children of the village. When I was Little Spoon and a pagan I have many times inflicted it on our captives, but that was before Blackrobe came to Teanaustayae and poured Saving Waters on my forehead. I remember our Iroquois captives would hurl curses at us. It was different here in the long lodge of Ossernenon that first night. What cries there were, came from the lips of my people as prayers and they did not wish out loud that similar torments would come on their enemies' bodies.

When Birch Bark went to his own lodge to watch the staked down captives there, my small guards bound my legs and arms to a lodge pole, so they might not miss their share in the cruelties.

They left, taunting me that my turn would come before the dawn. And it was here I had to watch Blackrobe strung up between two poles. This is a most painful position and when his agony became too intense, he begged his tormentors to loosen a little his bonds. They laughed and tightened his arm thongs. . . .

When my other father fainted away, they cut him loose and squaws dragged him back to stake him down again.

It was beyond half way between the going and the coming of the sun when I must have fallen asleep in my bonds. A shriek from one of the captives woke me.

All down the smoky length of the long lodge the Iroquois children were busy driving in the awls that hurt but do not kill, and dropping the hot glowing cinders on the naked flesh of the staked-down captives. The children's laughter, when the captive was not able to wiggle off the cinder was high and shrill. Most often the children's laughter came from the other end of the long lodge where were staked down Eustace, my father, René Goupil, and Blackrobe. . . .

But I was too tired to wake up fully and too sore to move. I did murmur a prayer of thanks to the Squaw in Blue that she had taken pity on my smallness and let me be tied aside and not staked down. I remembered it was after midnight and so the Feast of her Assumption.

Later, I remember it becoming lighter in the long smoky lodge and then more quiet. At length even the laughter of the children stopped. It was good to sleep. I, Tarcisius Tandihetsi, say so.

Chapter Ten

The Decision of the Council

THAT FIRST WEEK in the enemy's country had so many awful things crowded into every day and every night that I do not remember them all, but there does remain in my mind that hot morning we captives were dragged to Andagaron, another Mohawk village of four hundred fires.

When poor Blackrobe was lifted to the stage—to walk upright had become too difficult for him—there were there already prepared for execution four pagan braves from the Tobacco Nation. They had been taken by another war party some days before us. These braves were not nice to look upon.

One called to me in Huron. He said: "We wish to see him who prays and instructs. He came to our country last year."

When I told this to my other father he began to crawl over to where these four Tobaccos lay and their eyes lighted up when he spoke to them. With the clamor that the Iroquois made all about the stage I could not hear my other father's words, but I knew he was telling them of God and His beautiful country that awaited Christians beyond the flames in the long lodges that night. It is easy to think of that country when you are soon to go there. It makes you stronger against crying out or moaning when the pains come. I felt good that I was Tarcisius Tandihetsi and not the pagan Little Spoon that I had been before Blackrobe poured Saving Waters on my head.

I knew there was no water on the stage. I asked Straight Legs, an Iroquois imp who was yelling and screeching below me, for a drink of water. But the boy threw sand in my face and almost blinded me. I felt the flames of anger within me, but I remembered how my other father would act if this were done to him. So I changed the hot words that rushed to my lips into a silent prayer to the Squaw in Blue. Then I felt angry no more against the boy, Straight Legs. Feeling good that way, I felt better when I saw Partridge, the brave who had been in the canoe with me and who is cruel as a lynx, ordering some of the squaws of the village to give us captives corn. We had not eaten that day and if you do not eat you grow weak. I, Tarcisius Tandihetsi, know this.

The food these squaws brought to the stage in the middle of the palisaded village, was excellent. It was fresh corn and the green leaves still held some drops of last night's rain.

When I saw these leaves I took some that were sparkling with drops and brought them to Blackrobe. He tried to smile, but it was difficult, for his beard had all been plucked out that second night at Ossernenon.

"My Tarcisius is thoughtful and helpful and the Good God will reward him."

With his poor swollen hands that made him clumsy as a bear he gathered the leaf that held the rain drops and he shook some of the drops over the head of the first Tobacco.

Partridge sprang on the stage and he shouted evilly.

Then he called to the bound Tobacco captives: "You have no sense, brothers. Do you not know that a squaw of Andagaron died and she came back to one of our sorcerers with this warning: 'The Heaven of the Blackrobes is a place of torments. They pour Saving Waters on our heads that they may send as many as possible to their Heaven where they will torment and burn us at their leisure.' The Broad Breeches at Fort Orange tell us the same."

Partridge reached Blackrobe's side and with his war club he knocked the leaf out of his livid hands. But I was glad to see that my other father had poured Saving Waters on the second Tobacco before the Mohawk struck him.

I knew what Partridge said was a wicked lie and I made a face at the back of that bad Iroquois.

I felt better later that afternoon when the Iroquois were leading us to their largest village, Tionnontoguen, and we had to ford a stream. Here my Blackrobe got his tattered gown soaking wet and, before it dried, he managed to get near the two other Tobacco pagans and make them Christians.

All four Tobaccos were burnt that night; two at Andagaron and these last two before us as we lay bound in a long lodge of Tionnontoguen. These did not utter a moan of pain throughout the long hours of torture, even when the Iroquois held their fingertips in the pipes all red with heat. But they did cry out the Sacred Name and the name of the Squaw in Blue, as Blackrobe instructed them.

It strengthened me against my time to know I had helped Blackrobe to get the water necessary and I hoped these four Tobaccos would help me now that they were in the land of God.

Three days later when we had been paraded back to Andagaron and staggered up to the stage, that apostate, Snake Tooth, met us and he said: "Listen, dead men, the great council has been held. The calumet has been smoked and it is decided that you have suffered long enough. The captains have decreed mercy is to be shown to you. Look long into the west and see Sun. Remember each of you that it is the last time you shall see him."

He did not have to tell us more, for that is their way of notifying the captives that they are to be burnt over the slow fires of the Iroquois that night.

Then Snake Tooth left us on the stage and we could see below us the squaws preparing the war kettles in which they boil the flesh for the feast. . . .

The children of the village hurled sticks and stones, and Wild Berries and Jumping Rabbit shouted at me: "Stay with us, Little Spoon. We will embrace you like a brother. We will learn from you the Prayer of Ondesonk." And they blessed themselves as they saw the Christian captives do. These and other mocking things they shouted and did till the sun went out of the sky.

My other father seemed very happy that hot afternoon. Though he was not nice to look upon—which of us was after that week of Iroquois welcome?—he crawled about the stage. The confessions of all he heard.

I stayed with Eustace, my father, and he never was braver than when he lay bound and helpless there on the stage in the middle of this second village of our enemies.

He said to me: "Tarcisius, I am already a dead man, but because you are still a boy, they may yet spare you. If they should not, then remember these my words."

"What are they, Eustace, my father?" I asked.

"In the old days before the Blackrobes came to our village of Teanaustayae, when you were Little Spoon and I was Ahatsistari, The Hunter, I would have taught you to hurl curses on our enemies and to cry to your last breath these words: 'May an avenger arise from our bones. May Quick Death live in your village and may hunger gnaw your bellies. May there be no deer in your woods and no fish in your streams. May fire fiercer than these flames consume your squaws and your papooses. May——' Ah! But I begin to rave as the pagans do. Forgive me, little son of mine, as I hope He Who makes all things will. These are not the words I wish on your lips tonight in the long lodge of these people. No."

Here Eustace, my father, tried to caress me with his hands, but they were swollen like war clubs and he could only paw me clumsily, and his touch hurt me as it hurt him.

"No; little Tarcisius, you and I know this life is not longer than the tip of the fingers that they burnt in the hot pipes. These are not the words I wish on your lips in the flames. You and I have no enemies. So say, as Ondesonk has taught us, 'Jesus, have pity on the Mohawks. Jesus, I shall soon be happy in Your Heaven. Jesus, have pity on us.'"

Never did I like Eustace, my father, as I did then. There was great strength in those words of Blackrobe, and I almost began to wish that night would come quickly.

My other father crawled to my side now and I told my sins to him. It is easy to make a good confession when you know before the sun comes again you will have seen God and the Squaw in Blue.

Blackrobe spoke to all of us and he said: "Tonight, my children, we will be separated. So let us make now this sign."

Here he put his poor mangled right hand to his breast and raised his eyes to the blue sky.

"When you do this I will know you wish to say to me, 'Ondesonk, I desire Absolution.' As long as I am able, my children, I will give it to you, whenever I see you make that sign." And again he raised his eyes and tried to lay his hand on his raw breast.

Before black night came, White Oak, an old sorcerer, who had a red-stained headpiece and wore an apron with a painted sun on it, ascended our stage. He told us the council had again met and changed its decision.

I learnt that Eustace, my father, with seven others were to be burnt at Tionnontoguen; Paul Ononhoraton, and two more at Ossernenon. The council of Iroquois captains had decided that the white braves' lives and Blackrobe's were to be spared.

So was mine. But the slow fires of the Iroquois Mohawks might have been better, for with the falling of black night Birch Bark appeared and he told me that the slain Two Beavers' squaw, Who Has the Face Black, had offered beads of porcelain to the council and bought me for a slave.

I was led at once to her lodge in Ossernenon. Now, by Iroquois custom no person in the village could kill me, except Who Has the Face Black and her family.

It was when I saw that Curly Dog, who had been so cruel to my Blackrobe, was this squaw's son, that I wished the slow fires of the Iroquois had burnt me and I had gone to God, as did Eustace, my father, and half of the Christian Huron captives that terrible night.

Chapter Eleven

The Sign of the Cross

NOW THAT I had been bought into the family of Who Has the Face Black I received my first mercy in Ossernenon. This burly squaw covered my wounds with dressings of bark and herbs, that had previously been boiled, and wrapped them in leaves of corn. Who Has the Face Black had pity in her heart and she tried to make me whole again. Anyway, I was her property and it was only right that I be able to work as a slave boy should.

I was contented too. For my other father was a slave belonging to the family of Kicking Bear, who shared our fireplace in this long lodge. His mistress was Who Keeps the Kettle. She was Kicking Bear's father's squaw and was wrinkled and white-haired and seemed to have been old when old was young.

I could look across and see Blackrobe while we lay healing. But Who Has the Face Black interrupted him many times when he would speak with me. Then it was I would try to remember what Blackrobe said when we lay bound on one of the stages. "God uses the Iroquois as whips to make us have recourse to Him." Sometimes when I would think of Eustace, my father, and Catherine, his squaw, so far away, I would wish that God had used us Hurons as whips for these Iroquois. But when I said a prayer to the Squaw in Blue I did not think these thoughts any more.

Besides the cruel Curly Dog, Who Has the Face Black had another son. He was Wild Berries, the boy who had checked me when I ran the gauntlet. He did not like me, and once when I lay in the fever that burnt me, Who Has the Face Black caught him kicking me. I learnt how the Mohawks punish their children. It is different from our Huron custom. She caught the boy and holding him firmly, rubbed over his tongue and lips a bitter root.

Wild Berries had a wooly puppy he called Squirrel Chaser. While my wounds were healing up and Wild Berries was not in the smoky long lodge I would play with Squirrel Chaser and he would share all the food I received from the kettle. I liked Squirrel Chaser very much.

Then one afternoon a dreadful thing happened. Blackrobe was lying on an old skin across the fireplace from my compartment. His mistress, Who Keeps the Kettle, was dressing his wounds and Squirrel Chaser had waddled across and was trying to lick Blackrobe's face. I was grinning, when I heard shoutings that filled the long lodge. I looked, but the smoke was too thick to see far. Suddenly a wild figure of a Mohawk came over me. He brandished a tomahawk and his eyes were staring. He kept shouting: "I've had a dream from Sun. Where is Ondesonk? Where is the white sorcerer? Sun says to kill him—kill him—kill him!"

He looked around my compartment and then he leapt over the glowing coals of the fireplace. I saw he had no sense. Fear came into my heart and I thought my other father was going to God. But the old squaw, Who Keeps the Kettle, was not afraid. She stopped dressing Blackrobe's wounds and grabbed up Squirrel Chaser. The puppy yelped and that made more noise in the long lodge. The squaw stood in front of the glaring Mohawk and holding out the wooly puppy, said: "Here, Full Moon, put down your tomahawk. Sun has changed his command. He says kill this dog instead. He is a little thief, for he stole a piece of meat the size of himself out of my kettle. Let him be Sun's victim and you will please Sun."

The mad Mohawk, the squaw called Full Moon, stopped his shoutings. He lowered his tomahawk. "Who Keeps the Kettle speaks wise words," he said. He took Squirrel Chaser by the tail. The puppy yelped and I cried out too. Then the puppy's yelps stopped suddenly, and Full Moon began a chant to Sun. He bore the little body around the fireplace in triumph. I was very sad and yet glad that this mad Mohawk had not killed my other father.

Wild Berries came back and he was angry with Who Keeps the Kettle. The boy watched his chance and then he snatched the limp body from Full Moon's hand. He darted away, yelling shameful words at the mad man.

Later, Wild Berries brought the body back and dropped it into the family kettle and kicked me savagely.

Indeed, Blackrobe was right. God does use these Iroquois as whips.

That black night I missed Squirrel Chaser very much. I had to say prayers to the Squaw in Blue, for I felt very miserable and friendless within my breast. The thought came that I would prefer to lose Squirrel Chaser before Blackrobe. That is true. I, Tarcisius Tandihetsi, say so. I felt better and yet I reached over in the dark and petted the empty spot by my shoulder where the friendly puppy liked to sleep curled up in a warm wooly ball.

It was shortly after this time, when I was up again and able to go beyond the palisades of Ossernenon, to gather wood for the fires, that Wild Berries fell sick. All night he was moaning and by gray dawn he did not look in the least like the lively boy of yesterday.

As Wild Berries lay shivering by our fireplace in the long lodge, I saw the white brave, René Goupil, come by with his bundle of fagots for his master's fire. When he saw Wild Berries he stopped and smiled down on him. Then he went and threw his wood by his fireplace and came back. René Goupil, so my other father had told me, was a surgeon. It was to practice his skill in my village of Teanaustayae that he was coming with Blackrobe, when the Iroquois ambushed us on the Great River.

Goupil examined Wild Berries. I watched and the white brave said to me: "We must tell good Father Jogues here is another little one about to go to God."

"Blackrobe," I hastened to tell him, "is south of the palisades. I heard his mistress, Who Keeps the Kettle, order him to gather fagots there."

"Tarcisius, tell this child that I will not hurt him." René Goupil said this to me in broken Huron, for he was just learning my tongue.

"Wild Berries,"—I stooped and shook the boy vigorously, but he only turned fevered eyes on me. There was no look of hate in his features. I saw he did not recognize me.

René Goupil knelt down beside the mat of braided husks on which the Mohawk boy was stretched out. He drew down the deer-skin covering. Then he made the Sign of the Cross on the face and breast of the sick boy.

"I will go and seek Father Jogues," he said.

When Goupil disappeared in the smoke of the long lodge, I heard a movement in the next apartment and up rose the old sorcerer, White Oak, who is the father of Who Has the Face Black. He was very angry and the necklace of white-man's keys that he wore jangled.

He came to where Wild Berries lay.

"What Christian sorcery does that white dog do?" he demanded of me.

"He tried to help your grandson, White Oak, and make him well."

No sooner had I said this than he cuffed me and sent me spinning into a lodge pole. This he could do at pleasure as I belonged to his family.

"Go, Little Spoon," he thundered, "find my nephew Birch Bark. Tell him White Oak wants him to come here. I have spoken."

I went out into the village street to obey. I asked Jumping Rabbit, who was playing there with a clumsy bear cub that a hunter had brought in that morning: "Mohawk boy, did you see Birch Bark?"

But he mocked me, drawing the Sign of the Cross in the sand. Some of the other boys blessed themselves as they had seen us Christian captives do.

When I went on, they called after me: "See! Here is the Prayer walking about!"

I did not like that till I remembered again what my Blackrobe had said, "These pagans are but whips God uses to make us have recourse to Him." These jeering children were little whips.

By the south gate through the palisades where squaws were basket making, I found Birch Bark. He was fashioning a paddle. The tattooed snake on his breast gleamed in the sunshine.

He returned with me. The old sorcerer was angry. His words came quickly. "The white brave who is here with Ondesonk has been practicing his magic on my grandson. I hid and watched." White Oak pointed at Wild Berries.

"Their magic is powerful but evil," said Birch Bark. "Snake Tooth said at the council the Blackrobe and his companions do magic with water and signs on us to lead to their Heaven as many Iroquois as possible. There they mean to burn and roast us at leisure. It is bad medicine. Likewise, the Broad Breeches who come trading in our villages warn us to beware of their magic."

White Oak nodded. "They all should have been burnt as the Bear Clan voted." He continued: "I was here and I saw the white brave come and practice. He put this magic sign on the face of my grandson."

With this White Oak made a clumsy Sign of the Cross in the air.

"That is the sign. It is not good, as the Broad Breeches say." Birch Bark agreed and added: "I myself have seen this white brave make this sign on other children at their play. It is not good."

"It is good." I tried to explain, but Birch Bark grabbed me and, digging his long nails into my sides that were almost healed, opened a wound again.

"Huron puppy, keep your tongue in its kennel." Then he flung me to the ground and I almost fell into the fireplace.

When I got to my feet I heard White Oak ordering: "I fear lest some evil spirit will come upon my grandson from this sign. Go, nephew, kill that white dog."

When I heard this command of the old sorcerer, I ran out of the long lodge, for I knew White Oak was the master of René Goupil and he held the power of life or death over his slaves.

An arrow's flight beyond the western gate, I met the squaw Theresa, who had been captured with us and given to Partridge as his squaw. She was smoking freshly killed bear meat, but she stopped to tell me René Goupil and my other father were walking on the hill.

I rushed up through the woods. Just as I came to a clearing where I had sight of the River of the Mohawks far below, I came upon my Blackrobe and the white brave.

Quickly I told them White Oak's command.

René Goupil smiled as he turned and looked at Blackrobe. He cried: "Father, may God be blessed! He has permitted this! May His Holy Will be done!" And I saw him lift his hand to his breast and raise his eyes to the blue sky. I knew the signal. I stepped back as Goupil whispered into the ear of Blackrobe. I also blessed myself when Blackrobe's mangled right hand gave the Absolution.

Then my other father called me to his side.

"Come, Tarcisius, let us all recommend ourselves to Our Lord and your Squaw in Blue."

Blackrobe spoke to René Goupil: "And now, my dear brother, we have often asked Him to accept our lives and our blood for the salvation of these blinded people. Come, let us recommend ourselves confidently."

With this, Blackrobe took out his rosary, that Partridge had returned to him from the plunder of the canoes. René Goupil and I said our Hail Marys on our fingers.

We walked slowly down the hill towards Ossernenon. We saw Birch Bark and another young brave, who was called Two Noses, standing under a cedar.

"These two have an evil design," whispered Goupil.

"Keep on," counseled Blackrobe; "we are safe in God's Hands."

As we came up to the Mohawks, Birch Bark shouted an order: "Frenchmen, return to your long lodge at once."

My other father and his companion started to obey. When we came in sight of the western gate into Ossernenon and were just beginning the Fourth Glorious Mystery of our rosary, Two Noses told me to go back up the trail to the three cedar trees and see if his knife had fallen there.

I saw his knife concealed in his left hand, partly under the deerskin he wore. Before I could say anything Blackrobe told me to go, and, as I turned, René Goupil looked smilingly into my face. His eyes were very happy. I never forgot that look.

I ran back till a big oak hid me. Then I stopped in my tracks and looked back.

There was the worn trail leading into the village gate and smoke curling up from the long lodges. The mad Mohawk, Full Moon, was sleeping in the gateway. Children and dogs played their games under the shadows of the palisades. Blackrobe and René Goupil were walking towards the children and behind them came the two Mohawks. I knew Goupil had come to the Sacred Name in a Hail Mary from the reverent way he bowed his head.

Then Two Noses touched Blackrobe on the left arm and, as my other father turned that way, I saw Birch Bark's hand come out from under the deerskin he had over his shoulders.

There was the bright flash of a tomahawk, incredibly swift, out and down.

René Goupil fell forward and, his hands outspread before him, writhed like wounded black snakes.

It was done so quickly that Blackrobe was speaking to Two Noses and did not at first know.

When he saw his companion, Blackrobe fell on his knees and, sweeping off the cap he wore, looked up at the reeking tomahawk in the hand of Birch Bark. The sun was shining on his face. There was no fear there.

But Birch Bark waved him back and I remembered my other father belonged to another family. That was why Birch Bark could not kill him. I belonged to Birch Bark's family, but, recalling White Oak's command, I knew I was not to be murdered then.

I saw some of the Mohawk children had stopped their games for a moment, but seeing it was only a slave being tomahawked, they turned back to their play. Two of the dogs came sneaking up though.

When I ran forward, René Goupil lay quite still. Blackrobe, who was crying as I had never seen him weep under torture, threw himself on the body and kept calling, "René! My dear René! My happy René!"

Birch Bark would not let him stay long, for he ordered Blackrobe to get up and then he sent me away too.

"Ondesonk, go back to Who Keeps the Kettle. And you go along, Huron puppy, and tell White Oak what you have seen. Go."

Walking towards the gateway in the palisades, my Blackrobe kept weeping. He said to me: "Tarcisius, we have lost an angel of innocence, but you and I have seen a Martyr of Jesus Christ. Pray to René now for this darkened land. Always it is true the blood of martyrs is the seed of the Church."

I did not say anything, for I did not know what to say. It frightened me to see my other father crying like a squaw. He did not weep when he ran the gauntlet.

Yet when we got to the long lodge, Kicking Bear, Blackrobe's master, met us and he examined the red marks on my other father to see if he had been wounded. Then he put his hand over Blackrobe's heart to learn if it was beating faster.

"Your heart beats like mine," said Kicking Bear to my other father; "you are brave. But do not go out of Ossernenon, unless in company with one of my family. There are some young braves of the Bear Clan who are bent on killing you too. Be, then, on your guard."

When I got to my fireplace, I found Who Has the Face Black there and she was very happy. For Wild Berries was lively again and the fever had left him completely. Who Has the Face Black said it was the herbs that had killed the fever. But I knew better. And that black night, when I lay thinking over the day and what I had seen, I prayed the Squaw in Blue to keep watching me and I added another prayer to René Goupil, for he was a Martyr of Christ. This I, Tarcisius Tandihetsi, know.

Chapter Twelve

Honors to a Victor

WHO KEEPS the Kettle kept Blackrobe within the palisades all next day and it was well that she did so, for I saw Two Noses and two other young Mohawk braves watching our long lodge. When I told this to my other father, he said: "Tarcisius, you have the eagle's eyes. Use them and see how the Good God watches those who try to serve Him. No matter how cunning and crazy our brothers, the Iroquois, are they cannot harm a hair on our heads without His permission. Even the mad brave, Full Moon, could not. So you obey your master and I will obey my aunt." He had come to call his mistress, Who Keeps the Kettle, "aunt," for she was not cruel as some of the squaws.

I looked at Blackrobe and there was not much hair left in his brown beard, for our enemies had plucked it out most savagely. But I thought that He Who made all things had given them permission to do so. I knew also without much thinking why they had left the hair in his scalp lock and in mine.

Blackrobe must have read my mind, as he often does, for he smiled down on me.

"Say a little prayer to the dear Martyr we saw win to Christ's Side yesterday and then, as Who Has the Face Black has not forbidden you to go beyond the gate, go confidently and tell me what they have done with that precious body."

My other father must have seen the puzzlement in my face for he added: "Why does Little Spoon doubt? Of course, that body is

77

precious, the most precious thing in Ossernenon. For it is on such victorious bones that we priests offer the Holy Sacrifice."

I hung my head, because this was the first time my other father had called me by my pagan name since the capture.

But I went promptly. I saw Birch Bark and Curly Dog by the gate to the south, so I decided to look in another direction first. That murderous brave, Birch Bark, always made Devil come into my breast if I thought of him.

Beyond the northern gateway is a thick wooded ravine with a stream at the bottom of it, where I am sent to draw water for Who Has the Face Black's kettle.

I heard Iroquois children shouting and dogs barking, but a clump of sumac hid them from my sight. They were having great fun, of this I was sure.

I felt lonely inside my breast as I walked down the ravine, because I was not allowed to join in their games. I thought of the games in my village so far away and then I sighed, for it is not pleasant for a chief's son to be a slave and do squaw's work all day long.

But when I cleared the sumac and saw the kind of game the boys and girls and dogs of the village were playing I did not want to join in.

Some ten or twelve of the village children were there by the bank of the stream and they had René Goupil with a rope around his neck. They were marching up and down and they had been playing all morning. Jumping Rabbit with a stick was driving off the dogs. Village dogs are always hungry.

The boy pulling on the rope turned and I saw his face. It was Wild Berries. He was well again and having the most fun.

I spoke out loud and this time I did not care if my other father heard me or not.

I said: "I wish I had a bow and arrow, or better yet, a tomahawk."

And I swung my imaginary hatchet and brought it down deep

in the skull of that boy, Wild Berries.

Then I ran back till I came into the smoke of our long lodge. When Blackrobe heard all I had seen, I felt ashamed of what I had thought out loud and I confessed it to him.

He put his mangled hands on my shoulders and looking down at me as if he was not displeased, said: "Tarcisius, there is a better bow and arrow, and a sharper tomahawk than the one you would like to use on our little brother, Wild Berries. I use them often on my larger brothers of this village."

He laughed when I showed that I did not understand him at all.

"You remember Who it was Who said: 'Father, forgive them for they know not what they do?'"

"That was the Captain Christ on His Cross." I knew that from the lessons Blackrobe had taught me in my village of Teanaustayae far away.

"Christ on His Cross taught you and me how to bury our tomahawks in the skulls of those we do not like too much."

As our Huron custom is, I bowed my head between my knees. This means, I will not do so any more. And I murmured: "Then I'll say three Hail Marys today for Wild Berries. But, other father, they are going to hurt me in here." I touched my breast.

Blackrobe shifted his mangled hand from my bare shoulder and, placing it over my heart, let it rest. There came to me that feeling of peace and gladness that I always feel from the touch of my Blackrobe's hands.

"I am going to say four Hail Marys for that boy," I told him, "and ask the Squaw in Blue to make him want Saving Waters."

Who Has the Face Black called out sharply and sent me to carry an earthenware jar to another long lodge and I did not see Blackrobe again till the next day.

As soon as his squaw's work was done, my other father told me to come with him and we walked beyond the gate towards the clump of sumac near the stream.

Blackrobe's aunt met us at the head of the ravine. She was carrying a sack of corn from the fields.

She warned him: "Ondesonk, where are you going? You have no more sense than Full Moon. The young braves are waiting to take your life and you go hunting for a carcass already——"

"I have no fear, aunt," Blackrobe interrupted Who Keeps the Kettle.

As the squaw did not forbid him, we went on.

It was quiet beyond the clump of sumac and I guessed the children of the village were chasing a young deer that Wild Berries had sighted that morning in the woods west of Ossernenon.

Blackrobe and I came to the stream's side and there were the imprints of small naked feet and the marks of the dogs and the track where they had dragged René Goupil yesterday.

But though we searched in the water and all along the bank, we could not find the body. Just as Blackrobe was about to give up, I saw that lean yellow squaw dog of Wild Berries come sneaking out of some bushes, maybe an arrow's flight downstream.

I ran towards her. She bared her teeth at me, but Wild Berries was not about and so it was safe to throw a stone at her ribs. With a yelp she dropped her tail and fled for the palisades. I felt better within my breast.

I let her run and went towards the bushes.

Then I called to Blackrobe: "Other father, come here."

He began to weep many tears when he knelt and saw what was there. Most reverently, as though he was kissing the altar cloth on which rests the Body of Christ at Mass, he kissed this torn corpse.

"Poor René! Poor René!" Blackrobe kept repeating. And he tried with his mangled hands to lift the body. But those hands were not all healed yet and my other father had to let me help him.

Together we carried the body into the stream till the water was up to my breast, so that sometimes I had to swim. There was no current there. I got the heaviest stones I could carry and we weighted down René Goupil.

Blackrobe said: "When it is safer we will come back and give honorable burial to this blessed body."

The water was quite cold and my other father's teeth were chattering so when we waded ashore, that I could not understand what he was saying.

"My other father," I told him, "you come back to the fire's heat in our long lodge and be warm again."

Blackrobe stood on the shore and kept looking at that quiet eddy in the waters.

When I called him for the fifth time, he started up the hill for the gate.

When we were half way out of the ravine, I noticed a boy's shaven head peeping out from behind a tree. I pretended not to see anything, but when Blackrobe had entered the palisades, I came sneaking back as quietly as a thieving village cur.

There was Wild Berries with two other boys and they were wading in the eddy.

I did not tell this to my other father. But two days later, when Blackrobe and I were free to seek the stream in the ravine again, there was no trace of the body.

That Wild Berries has a split tongue, for I heard him tell Blackrobe that he knew nothing. And it was not till later that Wild Berries, boasting in my presence, betrayed what he and the boys had done that day we hid the body in the stream.

I told Blackrobe and we went to the spot in the woods, about half a league away from the stream.

All we found were several half-gnawed bones and a skull that had three holes in it. These Blackrobe gathered up most reverently and I dug a hole and we buried what was left of René Goupil at the base of a great white oak.

Blackrobe had me cut a cross in the oak and I did it.

I remember what my other father said as we walked back to the village.

"Some day, long after you and I are with God, these relics of a Martyr of Christ will be found and then honors will be paid them. Such honors as my Tarcisius and I would like to give them, but are not able."

I did not understand what my other father meant, for surely the Iroquois would not do so and who else in these awful lands in the south would? I, Tarcisius Tandihetsi, cannot answer that.

Chapter Thirteen

The Captain of the Day

THE EVENING of the day Snake Tooth and Curly Dog returned from another war raid along the banks of the Great River, I came back to the long lodge and found a group of sachems and braves in the compartment opposite to Who Has the Face Black's. They were squatted on the sleeping platform, smoking their long pipes and asking Blackrobe words of question.

I squatted near the circle and listened to Blackrobe telling about the first chief, Adam, and his squaw, whom God made. I had heard him tell that before in the cabin of Eustace, my father.

When Blackrobe finished, the old sorcerer, White Oak, spoke: "That is not what we Mohawks believe, Ondesonk. I will tell you. This is what I have learnt from our ancient men, when I was very young.

"You must know before there were braves and squaws on this earth, Sun was walking in his lands and he saw a tree that did not bear fruit. Sun was angry at this useless tree and with his strength, that is the strength of many bears, he grasped the tree and pulled it up by the roots."

White Oak went through the motions of doing this and then he pointed to the ground.

"A great hole went down through the bottom of the lands of Sun, where the tree had stood.

"One of Sun's captains had a squaw. She was as lazy as a village dog who has stolen the contents of a kettle. The captain wished to punish his squaw, so he pushed her into this hole and she fell and fell till she struck our earth. She gave birth to twin papooses and died. These papooses were a boy and a girl. They are our first ancestors.

"That is what our ancient men say. They are wise. I have finished."

All the other Mohawks, as their custom is, grunted their approval of White Oak's words.

While the old sorcerer was speaking, Snake Tooth and Curly Dog had come in. I noticed Curly Dog carried an otter-skin pouch. He carried it very carefully.

Now Curly Dog pushed forward. He put the pouch down. This is what I heard.

"Ondesonk, I know you speak words of wisdom and know the strange ways of the white men. There is something we of the village council do not understand."

"Speak it, Curly Dog," invited my other father, "and if I know it, I will tell you. There are many things I wish to tell you. That is why I am glad He Who makes all things let me come into your castles."

"This is it." Curly Dog lifted up very carefully the otter-skin pouch, that was secured with many deer thongs.

The circle of smoking Mohawks looked on gravely and I edged closer to Blackrobe.

"When Snake Tooth and I were on the bank of the Great River," Curly Dog continued, "we hid our party in the reeds below a rapids and saw a canoe that contained three white braves. These were paddling from the village of Three Rivers.

"We made our thunder-sticks speak first and the white braves fell across their canoe and did not rise. Among their bundles we found a strange animal. I know all the animals in the woods, but this is not like any of them. For it spoke, but now it is dead."

Here Snake Tooth said: "Ondesonk, it is an animal made of iron and it has the voice of a bell."

"It is a magic animal and will let loose Evil Spirits of the white men on our villages," objected Kicking Bear. "I voted at the council in the sachems' long lodge to drown it in the river. That is safer."

"Let me see it," said Blackrobe; "if it is of iron, it is not an animal. And if it was an animal and is now dead, how can it hurt you?"

I was very curious to see this strange animal and I crept forward and watched as Full Moon, the mad Mohawk, was told to open the otter-skin pouch. He has no sense and he does all that White Oak tells him.

At first I could not see, for the braves and squaws who had come about the compartment crowded forward. But many moved backwards as Full Moon untied the thongs. I heard my Blackrobe laugh, and then I knew within my breast that it was not a wild dangerous animal, like the lynx who lies along the branch, and it would not hurt anyone.

I heard my other father say: "White Oak, Curly Dog, all, so this is the strange animal you captured when you killed the three unfortunate Frenchmen! I think I can make it come alive if you give it to me."

Here Blackrobe's aunt, Who Has the Face Black, called out: "Do not touch it, nephew." And all the braves laughed. I did not, for I think that squaw was right.

Though my other father does not use magic like the wicked pagan sorcerers, his speech was very strange.

I wiggled myself forward till I could see over the shoulder of my Blackrobe and could spring up into the rafters if this was a dangerous animal.

There stood Full Moon, grinning the way those who have no sense grin, and holding in his hand the small dead animal. I had never seen anything like it in the woods.

I will tell you what it was like. It was not as large as a squirrel. It did not move—of this I am most sure. It had a body of iron, painted like a brave on the war trail, and a round white face with strange gold markings on it. There were four very short legs. It was the strangest animal I had ever seen. It did not look dangerous, but you never can tell about strange animals. It is best to kill them with an arrow or tomahawk first, and then examine them in safety. I, Tarcisius Tandihetsi, say so.

Blackrobe reached out his hand to take the animal, saying: "Give it to me, Full Moon."

But the grinning mad Mohawk held it tightly by the neck and would not give it up. Blackrobe now appealed to the old sorcerer: "White Oak, tell this Papoose Mind to hand the animal to me and I will make it come alive."

Some of the braves did not wish to let Blackrobe do so, but their curiosity won and finally White Oak commanded: "Full Moon, give it to Ondesonk."

At once the mad Mohawk obeyed the sorcerer. All the braves sat erect and the squaws leaned forward. I saw some of the braves were ready to leap and tomahawk the strange animal if it made a move to attack.

Blackrobe took the animal of the dead white braves and said: "Watch now, Mohawks, and listen."

Then while we watched breathlessly, my other father grasped the strange animal in his mangled hands. But he was too clumsy and he was not able to make it come alive.

Then he turned to me and he asked: "Tarcisius, you are not afraid to do what I tell you?"

"I am a chief's son and no squaw, other father," I replied, and though my heart was not afraid, I felt little quivers along my back as I took the strange animal.

"My poor hands are not healed enough to do my will," explained Blackrobe, "but do you, Tarcisius, turn that little tail that White Oak says is broken off. Put it back in place and twist it to the right."

I was going to tell my other father if I did that the tail would only break off again, but I took the queer tail, which certainly was of iron, like a kettle, and I put it back in its place and turned and turned as my other father directed.

Then a very strange thing happened. I, Tarcisius Tandihetsi, say so. The animal began to breathe loud and fast, so that all the Mohawks in the compartment could hear it. I saw Kicking Bear reach over his shoulder for his tomahawk.

Blackrobe took back the animal and I noticed that the long thin paws before the face of the creature were pointing; one to the ground and the other almost to the roof of the long lodge.

"Now, listen," said Blackrobe and he was smiling; "you will hear this speak."

It was so silent in the long lodge that all could hear the animal breathe. While we listened I myself saw the paw, that pointed to the roof, move very slowly, but it moved. The animal had come alive.

"Speak, clock," ordered my other father. He was smiling when he gave the command. But a few seconds later, while we all waited, the animal began to speak. It spoke one, two, three, four, five, six words and then it stopped.

"That is what it said in the white braves' canoe," explained Curly Dog, "Only more times."

"Where was the sun when it spoke," asked my other father. He was laughing.

"The sun, Ondesonk, was almost over head," gravely replied Snake Tooth.

"Then this must have spoken twice as many times. For this thing you Mohawks call an animal is an animal of time and it tells the hours when the sun has gone away."

"What does it say?" White Oak put this question.

"It says time is passing swiftly."

"It is wise, then," replied the old sorcerer.

"You speak its language, Ondesonk?" asked Kicking Bear.

"No; but I understand its language.

"Look!" Blackrobe put the tail back in the animal, and he very clumsily turned it till the hands almost stood over another mark on its face.

All the time the animal was breathing, but it never walked on its four short legs.

"Now, Mohawks, listen and see how obedient it is."

Blackrobe waited and then he commanded: "Speak."

Almost at once the animal began to speak again with a voice like strokes on a tiny bell.

When it was about to speak one more time than six, Blackrobe laughingly said: "That's enough." And the animal became silent.

All the Mohawks in the compartment were silent and smoked till White Oak spoke: "Ondesonk, we have seen this Captain of the Day come to life and we have heard it speak. It is a devil animal and will bring Evil Spirits on Ossernenon if it is let live. I said at the council it should be drowned and I say it again now. The white man has many devils work for him. They are not good."

The sorcerers agreed with White Oak. They made Full Moon put the animal back in the otter-skin pouch and tie it tight with deer thongs.

Snake Tooth and Curly Dog took it down the hillside and drowned it.

When I reported this to my other father, he laughed and shook his head. "These poor children! They listen to the devil who will hurt them and they destroy a clock that speaks to them only of God's time!"

I was alone now with Blackrobe and I asked him something that had puzzled me all evening.

"Other father, tell me one thing. Was that animal of the white braves, you called a clock, alive?"

"Little Full Moon!" exclaimed my other father, "it has no life as the squirrel and the beaver have. For a clock is made of iron like the rods and pots that the Broad Breeches trade to our brothers, the Iroquois, for their rich furs."

"I heard it begin to breathe! It began in my hands when I turned the tail!"

"Little Spoon! Little Spoon!" was all Blackrobe said, but I knew I had believed in pagan things and I bent my head between my knees to let my other father see that though I did not understand, I would not think so again.

Yet it was a very strange animal. I, Tarcisius Tandihetsi, say so.

Chapter Fourteen

Full Moon's Night

LATER THAT black night, when I was sleeping on my husk bed I heard a great outcry from the other end of the long lodge. Soon nobody could sleep with the shoutings.

I went with the other awakened sleepers and there we found Full Moon. He was crying and shouting and trembling. He was in convulsions, worse than I had ever seen a squaw's papoose.

Full Moon frightened all. When one who has no sense gets worse, the squaws run and hide all weapons, for such a one is very dangerous with a war club or a tomahawk. These Mohawks believe it angers Sun, their bad god, very much to kill one who has no sense. So they try to humor such a one.

While old squaws were heating a healing drink over the fireplace, Full Moon broke away from his father's squaw and leapt into the coals and lay there. He shouted more when Kicking Bear and the brave, Young Hawk, dragged him out.

They had to hold him tight and he shouted all the while about a dream Sun had sent him.

Braves held him till White Oak hobbled up. The mad Mohawk does all things the old sorcerer tells him.

I was as near as I could get and this is what Full Moon said: "In my dream an hour ago a white duck came and it carried that Captain of the Day in its bill, the strange animal of the white braves that you drowned a few hours ago in the river. The white duck dropped the Captain of the Day and hit me on the head with it.

Then the white duck plunged into my stomach, like one does when it is fishing in the river. It is there now and cannot get out."

Full Moon made pantomime to show White Oak what he dreamt. All the Mohawks listened and laughed.

Then White Oak examined Full Moon while the long lodge crowded around. I saw Wild Berries and Jumping Rabbit hanging to the rafters looking down. They were very much excited.

The old sorcerer straightened up and announced: "There is no duck in Full Moon's stomach."

"But there is, White Oak! There is!" repeated Full Moon, "it is saying, 'Quack! Quack! Quack!' and trying to straighten out its wings to fly."

The Mohawks all laughed: the squaws and the children the most.

The mad Mohawk was in earnest. Those who have no sense do believe such things.

So White Oak consulted with other sorcerers and finally he said: "That animal of the white braves was a devil, as I said at the council, and it has done this because Full Moon helped drown the Captain of the Day. We must cure Full Moon, or he will drown next time he goes in a canoe."

Here Full Moon's father's squaw began to cry.

White Oak gave orders and I watched the squaws hastily throw skins over poles and make a sweat box.

Then they offered Full Moon the hot drink with herbs in it. He cried: "No. No. Sun says pour it down the throat of the Huron boy, Little Spoon. For he made the Captain of the Day come to life again."

I did not like to hear such talk. Before I could sneak away Wild Berries leapt down from the rafters and grabbed me. Grinning braves helped him drag me forward.

White Oak said: "Huron slave, do as his dream commands. It will help to cure him."

I did not want to, but the Mohawks believe when one dreams anything, you must do as he says.

My mistress from the smoky background shouted at me to drink the hot drink. I struggled, for I do not want to do anything Sun, their bad god, says. But Full Moon's father's squaw poured the hot drink, which tasted very vile, down my throat till I choked and thought I would go to God that night.

White Oak watched my struggles and then he said: "That is good. Sun is pleased. Now Full Moon will do all that White Oak says to get the white duck out of his stomach."

Full Moon nodded his head and his friends laughed as squaws led him to the sweat box.

When only his head showed above the skins, squaws put stones, heated red hot from the fireplace, underneath and they poured water on these to make hot white clouds.

Then all the Mohawk braves and squaws and children in the long lodge began to dance around the sweat box. They held their stomachs and cried:

"Quack! Quack! Quack!" and flapped their arms like wings in flying.

I did not feel well, for that hot drink was very vile, when Blackrobe came up. He was laughing and when I watched the Iroquois I had to laugh too at some of the fat ones who waddled like ducks anyway when they walked.

This "Quack! Quack! Quack!" dance kept up for many minutes. Sometimes they would stop and then White Oak would ask Full Moon: "Has the white duck gone out yet?"

The mad Mohawk would say "No" and all would dance and shout "Quack! Quack! Quack!" again.

Finally, Full Moon cried out from the sweat box that he was perspiring too much. Then the Mohawks stopped their duck dance. White Oak came to the skins and asked: "Has the white duck gone out?"

"Yes; it has," said the mad Mohawk. "It went up through the smoke hole in the roof."

"Then you come out, Full Moon, and go to sleep. Sun has cured you."

Squaws lifted the skins off and Full Moon came out into the firelight. He was dripping as though he had fallen into the River of the Mohawks. But he was not trembling now.

His father's squaw led him to his compartment and he went most obediently.

Then it was quiet again in the long lodge.

When I went back to my compartment Wild Berries was very much excited and he explained to me: "That Full Moon, when his father's squaw was not watching, once ate the liver of a dog."

"What is wrong with that?" I asked the Mohawk boy.

"Little Spoon, you have no sense too," he jeered at me. "Do you not know that if anyone eats the liver of a dog his skin will fall off or his brain will rot? There was a young brave in Andagaron who did this when he was very hungry, and all his skin fell off before he died. Full Moon's skin is whole, but his brain has rotted away. That is why he has no sense."

I lay down thinking over what Wild Berries had said. I did not think his tongue was split then. In the morning I intended to ask my Blackrobe words of question.

I did not know if this was so or not, but before I fell asleep I said a prayer to the Squaw in Blue to keep my brain from rotting like Full Moon's. And I made a resolution never to eat the liver of a dog, even if I was starving in the snows at deer time. I, Tarcisius Tandihetsi, say so.

Chapter Fifteen

The Cat Boy

I HAD BEEN in the fields all that day keeping the thieving crows away from the corn as my mistress, Who Has the Face Black, ordered. I was tired and within my stomach there was a voice calling and calling for food. I was used to that voice now. Unless the hunters came back with meat we slaves ate little but the berries we gathered.

Then I felt not only hungry but lonely when towards the going down of the sun I came back towards the palisades of Ossernenon with a heavy load of fagots. For there beyond the southern gate, where the children of the village play, were Wild Berries and his companion, Jumping Rabbit, and many other boys.

They were playing Shoot Dart. They let me watch them. You know, they divide into two war parties and one side rolls a small hoop; one just wide enough to go over my head without touching either ear. When this hoop is rolling along the ground all the boys on the attacking side aim their small bows and each shoots a dart at the center of the rolling hoop. The dart has to go through or the other side wins it.

I saw Wild Berries was the best of the boys at Shoot Dart. Never once did his dart fail to go through and he would not stop to aim but bring his little bow up and pull, the way the braves did. He will be a mighty warrior some day and I could not help thinking that many of my tribe to the north would fall under his skill when he was tall enough to join the war parties.

Now I wished very much to join the village boys in this game, for in my village of Teanaustayae I also practiced with bow and dart. And my aim was true, like Wild Berries', for I have an eye like an eagle. Catherine, my father's squaw, would say that some day I would be mighty in war. Then I thought of my captivity. But this thought I put away with a prayer to the Squaw in Blue. It is not good for a slave boy to think such thoughts. My other father does not, and he is the bravest man I ever met; except Eustace, my father, of course.

When I was turning away to carry the bundle of fagots to Who Has the Face Black, the Iroquois boy, Jumping Rabbit, called me, saying: "Little Spoon, come here quickly."

When I came he held out a torn book. This I recognized at once as one that Blackrobe had in his baggage on the Great River. I remembered the afternoon when the squaw in charge of the virgin girls in the long convent at Quebec had given me a big piece of French cake that was very satisfying, and at the same time she gave Blackrobe this book.

My other father could make words come out of the pages.

Jumping Rabbit asked me: "Can you make this speak, Huron puppy?"

"I do not hear with my eyes," I told him, "but Blackrobe makes it speak and say words of God."

"Then it is a Manitou?"

"No; Mohawk boy, it is not a Manitou, but give it to me and I will carry it to Blackrobe and later I will tell you what it says."

I suspected that Jumping Rabbit had stolen it from the compartment of one of the Iroquois who had looted our Mission bags. I did not think Jumping Rabbit would give it to me, but just then the conch shells began to blow and at the sound all the village children dropped their bows and darts and raced for the hillside.

Sadness and pain were coming to some more captives that afternoon.

I picked up the book that makes speeches about God, intending to give it to Blackrobe. He was not in the long lodge of Who Keeps the Kettle, but I searched and found him in the long lodge of Partridge.

When I came up there was Theresa, Partridge's squaw, and another squaw. This other squaw held a papoose who was crying with powerful sounds.

Said Theresa: "Let the Blackrobe quiet him. He does no harm."

"Ondesonk must not touch him," the other squaw objected, "he will put some evil on my little Screech Owl."

Before Theresa could speak, my Blackrobe said smilingly: "Then if you fear my poor hands, I will not touch your little one. But do this and see if Screech Owl does not feel better."

My other father beckoned me forward and, taking my right hand, he made with it the Sign of the Cross on my forehead and shoulders and stomach.

The other squaw looked at her papoose who was in pain and then she timidly took its little hand and made the Sign as my other father had done on me.

I, Tarcisius Tandihetsi, say it because I saw it. For when the squaw finished, Screech Owl stopped crying with powerful sounds.

I had not heard her come in, but from beyond the fireplace, Who Keeps the Kettle spoke: "My nephew, you will cause your own death. You speak and act too boldly. It was the making of that Sign that caused your companion's death. If Young Hawk, the father of that papoose had been in the long lodge you would have been tomahawked next time you went beyond the palisades."

But Blackrobe, though he listened attentively to his aunt, shook his head and said: "My life hangs by a thread overlong. I will do in life what I would wish to have done at my death."

When we were alone I gave my Blackrobe the book that makes speeches about God, and his eyes lighted up as I had not seen them shine in many days.

"This book is my delight, Tarcisius. It is called the *Imitation of Christ* and from it, as from the lips of a beloved teacher, I have learned many lessons. It is a golden book—a golden book."

I could not see how that was so, for there was no gold on the binding or pages. But Blackrobe was sitting by the firelight and with inflamed and streaming eyes he was making this book speak to him. He forgot all about me.

I played with a friendly puppy, that was not as nice as Squirrel Chaser, and then as the shoutings came nearer I went out to see the captives on the stage.

There were eight of them. They were of the Nation of the Cats. Seven were all open wounds, as we had been that afternoon of our arrival at Ossernenon.

One captive was untouched. It was evident he had not run the gauntlet. He was a boy of about fourteen. I had never seen a boy as handsome as that Cat boy. All the squaws were talking loud words about his beauty. They said he looked like a god—like Sun.

As I watched and listened I learnt that the seven would be burnt that night in the other Mohawk villages, but the sachems of Ossernenon were even now in the council lodge, debating the boy's fate.

Then Curly Dog came and ordered squaws to bring out an elk robe, handsomely painted and trimmed with bright blue beads of porcelain. This the squaws fought to put on the Cat boy and he was made to parade up and down. Then he danced, and all the while the squaws were saying loud words about his beauty. This made some of the braves jealous and when the council re-met, they voted the boy an enemy to be burnt that night in Partridge's long lodge.

When I heard this handsome boy would die with the other Cats, I sought Blackrobe. He called my cousin, Bernard Atieronhonk, who speaks the language of these Cats, and he told him to tell the boy of the Prayer.

Bernard made objections to Blackrobe: "The Cats are our enemies as the Mohawk Iroquois are. Why then your Saving Waters on a Cat? He will go to Heaven before us and try to turn us out."

I knew that Bernard carried Devil in his heart, and my other father told him so.

Then Bernard went humbly to the handsome Cat boy, who was bound in the long lodge of Partridge, and Blackrobe spoke to him through Bernard's mouth.

The handsome Cat had heard of the Prayer from Huron captives in his nation and he listened to all Bernard's words.

Once I told Bernard to say: "Cat boy, when in the hands of the Iroquois the torments last but one night. In Hell they burn throughout all eternity."

The handsome boy replied and Bernard translated:

"This Cat, he says a Broad Breeches hunter who came to their village with thunder-sticks in each hand warned his people to beware of the words of Ondesonk, but now he says, to tell Ondesonk that something within his breast tells him that Ondesonk would not use split words to one who is already dead. He says that Broad Breeches used split words to his father and robbed him of many pelts. He does not believe the Broad Breeches' warning. So this Cat, he says, he believes Ondesonk's words and he wishes Saving Waters."

Then Blackrobe instructed him through Bernard's mouth and I brought water in Theresa's earthenware jar. Blackrobe poured it on the Cat's forehead.

That night the Mohawks tortured the handsome Cat in the long lodge of Partridge and because of his youth, the squaws insisted that they burn him only two hours.

Never did he moan, but once he looked at Blackrobe and said words in his strange tongue. Bernard translated: "Ondesonk, this young Cat, he says he will be happy in Heaven."

Chapter Sixteen

Dirk De Witte

NE BITTER DAWN after snow came I had brought in fagots for the fireplace and was seeking Blackrobe, when Who Has the Face Black sent me to Birch Bark. She told me to do what he commanded. I found him before his long lodge. He had his moose skins on and his snowshoes were slung over his back.

His leggins looked peculiar and coming closer it made me sad within my breast to see they were made from the veil for a chalice that had been in the bags of Mission supplies taken at our capture. Birch Bark's squaw had cut the veil and sewed a line of deer hoofs down each side. It is not right to use a chalice veil so, and I made a resolution in my breast to take those leggins if I got the chance and bury them deep. Later, I had the chance and I did and Birch Bark never found them again.

When Birch Bark saw me standing before the entrance to his long lodge he pointed to a pair of small snowshoes and he barked at me: "Huron puppy, take them and that bundle of jerked meat there and walk behind me."

We passed Blackrobe. He was with a group of small Mohawks. As his custom was, he was teaching the children to draw the Names "Jesus" and "Mary" in the snow.

I would have liked very much to speak with him, but Birch Bark would not allow me to stop.

Joining a snowshoed party at the west gate of the palisades, I learnt we were leaving Ossernenon to prepare for deer time.

99

We tramped for hours. Once the pagans halted where the trail swung around three gaunt oaks, and there at the trailside were two round stones. Each pagan sought till he found a small twig. Then, as is their superstitious way, the hunter threw it on the stone, saying out loud by way of homage: "Here is something to pay my passage that I may proceed in safety and track many deer and elk and moose."

None of the Christian slaves did this, of course. But I looked up into the blue skies and I said in my heart: "You Who make all the animals, send us meat for we are hungry." That is the prayer Eustace, my father, used to say at deer time. It is a much better prayer than one to two pagan stones. I, Tarcisius Tandihetsi, say so.

After the sun was overhead we came to Tionnontoguen, the largest palisaded village of these Mohawks. Many hunters were meeting here to track the deer. These Mohawks talked and smoked much while the slaves cleaned the snow from the place for the cabins. I dragged heaps of spruce branches that the squaws cut down. These are for sleeping mats. Very swiftly the squaws make cabins in deer time. Sheets of bark are stripped from trees. The cold makes this easy. This bark is thrown over poles stuck in the ground either side and made to meet. The cabins are open against the wind. In this open space big fires are lighted. But sometimes it is not any warmer within these hunting cabins than outside.

When my work was done Birch Bark let me go free. Here beyond the palisades was a plain where much snow had fallen and been crushed hard. The boys of Tionnontoguen were gathered together here to play the game they call Snow Snake.

This game is different from any that we Huron boys play. But I like it. The players line up and each has a small bundle of hickory sticks about as tall as Blackrobe. Each one in his turn throws along the crust of the snow and the boy whose stick goes farthest wins all the other sticks.

Wild Berries was in our party and he and I happened to come to the field together.

There was a boy hurling his stick as we came up. He was not an Iroquois, for his hair under his beaver cap was fair and his skin was not copper colored. He wore wide deerskin breeches and a fringed deerskin shirt. He had a pleasant round face and he was laughing as his stick sailed through the air. Mohawk boys always look serious when they play.

I liked this boy at once and came closer to watch. He could not hurl his hickory stick nearly as far as the Iroquois boys. But he laughed when he lost his last stick. Then he came over to where Wild Berries and I were standing, as strange boys will, at the side of the frozen field. The boys of Tionnontoguen paid no attention to us.

He spoke to Wild Berries and said: "Mohawk Iroquois, you do not belong to this village. You belong to Ossernenon."

Wild Berries told him: "That is correct and you are the son of the Broad Breeches trader at Fort Orange on the River of the Naked Bear (Hudson)?"

"I am Dirk De Witte. My father is now trading in the long lodge of the sachems."

Here he turned his laughing eyes, that were blue as porcelain beads, on me. There was a question in them and I read it.

"No; I am not an Iroquois. I am Tarcisius Tandihetsi, and my father was Eustace Ahatsistari, a brave Christian Huron captain, whom these pagans burnt here in this village."

"Yes; I think I remember him. I was here with my father when that Huron chief burnt. He was a very brave man. He did not cry out in the midst of terrible sufferings, but he did pray."

I smiled at the Broad Breeches boy when I heard him say these words.

Dirk De Witte called to one of the players who had won many hickory sticks and he took a handful from the winner. He gave five to Wild Berries and five to me, saying: "I cannot compete with these boys at Snow Snake, but maybe I can do better against you two."

Wild Berries was eager to show his skill and he snatched up the bundle of sticks.

We cast many times the sticks and we discovered that there was not the length of a papoose's little finger between the three tips. Again and again our three sticks would lie on the snow's crust with their points almost on a line.

This made Wild Berries mad, for he did not like to see a Broad Breeches and a Huron slave boy equal him in this Iroquois game. But I felt good within my breast at the sight and I tried harder. The next time we hurled at Snow Snake my stick was the length of an arrowhead beyond Wild Berries.

My face showed how glad I was.

"Huron puppy," cried Wild Berries, "who taught a dog like you to play Snow Snake?" And he said many other things about the Prayer which I will not repeat.

I watched him ready to guard myself and I walked towards my hickory sticks. I was not in Ossernenon now.

Dirk De Witte kept near Wild Berries and his fists were clinched. His blue eyes were not smiling.

All of a sudden Wild Berries stepped in to Dirk's side. The Broad Breeches threw up his hands to guard his head and as he did so, the Iroquois boy snatched the knife that was sheathed in Dirk De Witte's belt.

With this gleaming in his hand, Wild Berries rushed at me. A prayer to the Squaw in Blue came to my lips and then all in the same breath there came to me on the white snow there, the trick the white brave, René Goupil, had taught me to disarm an enemy.

As Wild Berries came in, instead of turning and running like a village dog, as he expected a Huron captive to do, I stepped in, caught his knife hand in a sharp twist and the knife fell to the frozen ground. The Broad Breeches dove and slid for it and Wild Berries howled with pain. I had meant that twist I gave his arm.

For many days I had wanted to fight with Wild Berries and then I forgot I was Tarcisius, a slave, and for the next five minutes I was Little Spoon and we tore and clawed at each other like lean village dogs over a bone. Dirk De Witte and the other boys and girls cheered us on.

I had Wild Berries down and was feeling to gouge out his eye, when I was pried off. . . .

After I got my breath I saw the white brave, William Couture, had done this. I was very angry that he had to come up at that time. I did not wish to stop, for Devil was in my heart and I wished most sincerely to slay Wild Berries. That was not the right desire for a Christian. It was some time before I could get that bad wicked desire out of my breast.

William Couture walked me away, saying: "You are very foolish, Little Wild Cat. That Mohawk cub very likely richly deserves it, but if you had hurt him, how long do you think you would have lived? A captive has no rights. Have you not learnt that during these long months? I have here at Tionnontoguen."

Then he asked for Blackrobe and when I told him all, he concluded: "I had hoped very much that he would have come with the hunting parties. You may yet meet him with some hunters from Ossernenon. Remember now these are my words and give them to Father Jogues when you see him. Say, 'Blackrobe, William Couture says try to escape. As soon as he learns that you are free, he will manage to get off. His master is friendly and will let him go in peace.' Can Tarcisius remember all that?"

I repeated his message word for word and told this white brave that I would hold it fresh in my heart till I met Blackrobe again.

By this time we had walked to the open space before the stage of Tionnontoguen, where the doomed captives lie. William Couture had to go to his master's long lodge and he left me.

I saw a group of the hunters. They played another game. This was most exciting and it made me forget Wild Berries.

In the ground was a stake no thicker than my wrist. There was a circle ten paces wide and four tomahawks lay at equal distance about this circle. The Mohawk hunters would start shouting and run around; sometimes only once, sometimes maybe five times. All would yell and give their barking war whoops. Then one of the runners would stoop and pick up a tomahawk. He would hurl it at the stake. As soon as he did, the three runners nearest to the other tomahawks would swoop down like hawks and sweep up the tomahawks and sail them at the stake.

I watched them do this many times and only once did a tomahawk fail to stick in the sides of the peg. This was Birch Bark's and the edge of his tomahawk was buried in the ground beside the peg. All the rest of the braves jeered him and called him names of squaws.

Birch Bark was so mad that he placed the four tomahawks at equal distance. Then he ran around twice and picking up the tomahawks, one after the other, he sank all four in the different sides of the peg. The circle of hunters did not jeer him now.

Birch Bark saw me watching and he called me over to him. Someone pushed me and I came unwillingly. My master ordered me to stand by the side of the palisades. There was a strip of bark fastened there. Quickly the Mohawk hunters bound my arms and my legs to the bark so that I could only move my head.

Here Wild Berries pushed through the crowd and whispered something in Birch Bark's ear. My master pushed the Mohawk boy aside and gathered up the four tomahawks.

"Huron puppy, keep your eyes on me," he directed.

I felt I knew what he intended to do, but if Wild Berries, grinning evilly from the crowd, thought I would show fear and beg, he was wrong. I am Tarcisius Tandihetsi, a chief's son. So I looked at Birch Bark right in the eye and I said: "You need not have bound me. I will not run away."

Birch Bark walked ten paces away and then turning as a bird does in the air, the Mohawk hurled the tomahawks, one, two, three, four.

All four buried themselves in the bark; one above and one below each ear, so my head was pinned firmly to the bark. Though they were close enough to touch me, yet none had drawn blood.

After that none of the crowd jeered at Birch Bark.

A fur-clad squaw unpinned me. She felt of my heart, but it was not beating any faster than usual. This made her whisper: "Huron slave, you are brave."

The squaw did not tell me what I did not know. I, Tarcisius Tandihetsi, say so.

Chapter Seventeen

Moose and Bear

NEXT MORNING we started for the deer. I did not see William Couture again before we left. Wild Berries did not come along and Birch Bark told me, when I asked him: "Huron puppy, you make him sick. He thought you would put your tail between your legs and run yelping away when he came at you. But watch out for my nephew when next you meet."

But I did not fear Wild Berries any more.

We traveled on our snowshoes twenty leagues to a country west of the Mohawk palisades. The deer were plentiful. So were the elk and the big moose. They were easy to track in the snows. The hunters killed many animals. We slaves helped the squaws make the cabins. Each night I ate from the kettles so that I could not eat any more. You do not mind the cold when you have plenty of meat in your stomach. I have noticed that. By day the squaws smoked much meat and I was kept very busy by Who Has the Face Black.

One day Curly Dog brought down a large moose and it was dragged near our cabin. I helped my mistress remove all the bones and stretch upon poles the two sides of the great animal. We had to raise the carcass in strips and slash it so the smoke would penetrate and dry all the parts. Then I had to pound the strips with stones till my arms ached, and tramp the strips under foot so that no juice would remain to spoil the moose meat. When the meat was thoroughly smoked I helped fold and make packages of it. This is squaw's work and I did not like to do it.

But when black night came work stopped and I liked this time for I could watch the young hunters play their games.

Once when they were playing Throw Knife in the fire light, I saw Curly Dog do a wonderful thing. In Throw Knife a pole that is used to smoke carcasses on is stuck in the ground at an angle. From the end of this pole is dropped a thin thong. A stone no larger than a squirrel's skull is fastened to the end of this thong. This hangs a foot from the ground. The young braves stand off five paces and in turn throw their hunting knives to cut the thong nearest to the stone. Sometimes their sharp knives only nick the thong, and the stone still hangs. Then all the watchers jeer and call names of squaws.

A Mohawk, not from Ossernenon, and Curly Dog had twice cut the thong so close that the stone fell away with no bit of thong about it. Then to settle the tie between them, a captain set the thong swinging back and forth rapidly. The strange Mohawk missed. None of the braves crowding about jeered at him, for this is a most difficult shot. But they shouted loudly when Curly Dog's knife cut the swinging thong neatly, only an inch above the stone. I shouted too. That was a most difficult shot. And after the games I told Curly Dog so. He grinned. I like him better than Birch Bark. It is too bad he is not a Huron. But when I told him this, he did not grin any more, and I went to the other side of the fireplace.

All this smoking of meat brought the wolves, whole packs of them, around our cabins. They kept just outside the light of the fires. Their howls of hunger are not pleasant sounds at black night. The hunters had to watch, and one night gray wolves got so bold they pulled down two watchers, who must have fallen asleep by the fire. One was the strange Mohawk, not of Ossernenon. His screams woke me and I remembered for a long time afterwards those cries in the cold, still darkness.

Next morning some of the packages of smoked meat were

sent back to Ossernenon on the backs of captives and squaws. I expected to be sent back in one of these parties, but Who Has the Face Black kept me with her.

Then Birch Bark received the wound hunting a bear. I saw it all. This bear was sleeping his long sleep in a hollow tree. It was very cold. The hunters felled the tree and as the bear came scrambling out of the trunk, Birch Bark rushed in among the branches to thrust his knife home. But he slipped on the icy ground and slid under the bear's claws.

Curly Dog hurled his tomahawk and it wounded the bear in the shoulder. This made the animal very angry and he scraped Birch Bark, tearing the muscles of his thigh, so that he could never walk straight again.

My master was in much pain for days but he made no sound. Who Has the Face Black nursed him till the sorcerers came. They had him carried back to Tionnontoguen, the largest Mohawk village. I was left to attend to him. Birch Bark, when he learnt that he would never go on war parties to the Great River again, seemed to get the temper of a wounded bear. He tossed on the sleeping bench of the long lodge and he was very cruel to me. I wished sometimes that I might go to God soon.

Came Spring and I began to think I would never go back to Ossernenon and see my other father. Once I met the white brave, William Couture, and he told me captives said Blackrobe was on a fishing trip with his aunt to the River of the Naked Bear. That was in the other direction from Ossernenon and I knew I would have no chance of meeting him. And I wished to very much.

When the cruel Birch Bark was able to walk, he limped, for the muscles of his thigh were all knotted. He was not the active brave I remembered, who moved like a young deer. He crept about like the old sorcerer, White Oak, who has the rheumatism. And I kept out of his way. He might have killed me.

It was summertime when we started the return. I had gladness in my heart for the first time in many moons. I would see my other father again.

But the afternoon we came within sight of the palisades of Ossernenon, I was weary, for Birch Bark had to use my shoulder as a cane. Then sadness came to me, for we met a party of Broad Breeches on horseback and with them were the trader, De Witte, and his blue-eyed son.

Dirk remembered me and, leaping down from his horse, he led me aside and there said: "I have a message for you. It is four-weeks' stale. The Blackrobe, Father Jogues, whom the Mohawks did not burn, but made a captive slave, has escaped."

"Back to the country of the Great River?" I asked. Dirk shook his head and then looking around to see if anyone overheard him, whispered: "Our good minister, Domine John Megapolensis, says Father Jogues is a martyr of Jesus Christ. So he has helped him and he is hidden at present in a farmer's house near our Fort Orange. The savages of Ossernenon are eager to get Blackrobe back. They desire to burn him at the stake because the French killed nine warriors of a raiding war party. I wish they had shot the whole party."

"So do I," I whispered back.

"But our Commandant swears he will not give Father Jogues up. He is to be shipped down the river to New Amsterdam and then across the ocean to France."

I did not understand all that Dirk said, but I knew these places were far away, like the stars.

"When does the Great Canoe take Blackrobe away?" I asked, and sadness filled my heart. For now I knew I would never see my other father again.

Here Dirk reached up and pulling down his horse's head, spoke in the animal's ear: "'Jan,' if I tell you something will you retell it to every Mohawk dog you meet?" Dirk seemed to be listening. It was something of no sense that he said, such as the mad Mohawk, Full Moon, might say and I was about to say so to the Broad Breeches boy. Then I saw Dirk looking straight at me, and I understood the words of question he addressed to the horse, "Jan," he meant for me.

Very serious I said: "Broad Breeches' horse, around the lodge fires I will forget all that you have told me. This I promise you, 'Jan,' if your master will trust me. For I greatly wish to see my Blackrobe before he sails in the Great Canoe."

Dirk grinned and, giving his horse a pat, said: "Wise Little Spoon, go to sleep each night in your compartment of the long lodge, but when Partridge's squaw, Theresa, wakes you, come and I will be waiting. Do not tell any of these painted Mohawks what I have told you. I do not care to roast. It is because your Blackrobe is also my friend that I promised to tell you, when word came that Birch Bark and his slave were returning."

All the slow way into Ossernenon I was silent, for I was thinking how I might get to Fort Orange on the River of the Naked Bear and see my other father again. That night in my prayers I asked the Squaw in Blue to show me the way, and I slept heavily, for I knew she would not fail me. I, Tarcisius Tandihetsi, say this.

Chapter Eighteen

Jan and the Wolves

IT WAS NINE days later before the opportunity came that I had been watching for. Then it was in the middle of the night. I had been sleeping soundly in Who Has the Face Black's compartment of the long lodge. The fires burnt low. The old sorcerer, White Oak, who was sick with his rheumatism again, lay on his mat of corn husks just beyond the light. I heard sudden yells from the next long lodge and then I was awake. I remembered all. A war party had come in with three captives from the Cats. They had run the gauntlet in the afternoon and had been left on the stage till after dark. Now the burnings were going on that would not end till the coming of dawn.

I sat up. I heard some dogs growling in their sleep. It was very still in our long lodge. The thought came to me as though someone had spoken that most of the Mohawks would be crowded into the long lodge for the burnings.

A small figure moved by the entrance and a dog barked. I rolled over till I was in the shadows and watched. The figure walked boldly through the smoke. I thought it was Wild Berries. But I did not fear him. I had a knife now.

Then I heard my name whispered: "Little Spoon."

It was not the voice of Wild Berries.

"Who are you?" My hand covered my knife and with my thumb I felt the keen edge. That makes you feel more secure. I, Tarcisius Tandihetsi, say so.

111

Then I sprang up and sheathed my knife as the figure whispered: "Dirk De Witte."

He dropped down on my mat and came crawling into the firelight. He crept closer. I saw he was stripped to Mohawk costume.

When he lay by my side he said: "I hid when my father went back this evening to Fort Orange, for I knew his Iroquois customers would all be at the Cat burnings. I hoped you would keep away. I tried to find Partridge's squaw, but could not."

"Theresa is away at the fishing place. Why did you come here yourself? You know if any of the Mohawks catch you prowling about their long lodges, they would——"

"They know me and they would not dare touch me. They desire the things my father has to trade for their peltries. And they fear the arquebuses of our Dutch too much. But we can talk better on our way. If you wish to see your Blackrobe, come now."

"I have wished that for many moons."

I followed him silently out of the smoky long lodge. Afterwards, I had good reason to think White Oak was not sleeping as soundly as he seemed.

A village cur growled, but retreated when I made a gesture at him with my knife. The yells of the Mohawks about their victims across the village street drowned any noise the dog made. Amid the yells of the children, I thought I recognized the shrill cries of Jumping Rabbit.

Dirk and I slipped through the small opening in the palisades that the boys use, and began to cross the moonlit plateau above the river.

A league east of Ossernenon, after we waded and swam the cold stream that empties into the River of the Mohawks, Dirk stopped in a thicket and there was his horse, "Jan," picketed. And in the bushes were Dirk's clothes.

While his small master slipped into his broad breeches and shirt, the horse whinnied with delight.

Then Dirk De Witte said: "Get up behind me and we will be in Fort Orange before noon."

It was clear moonlight and we followed the trail that I recognized the Mohawks traveled to put their nets in the River of the Naked Bear at fishing time.

On the way I clung to Dirk's waist. I am not used to riding on the back of a horse. It is very uncertain. I, Tarcisius Tandihetsi, say so.

Dirk spoke over his shoulder and told me more about Blackrobe. He had gone with his aunt fishing and the Commandant of the Broad Breeches post had persuaded him to escape.

Dirk said: "Father Jogues was bitten by one of the post dogs while he was trying to push his canoe into the water. Finally, he got out to the sailing boat and the Mohawks came demanding the captain give him up. He would not, and a funny thing happened to Young Hawk, who was in the party."

Here Dirk laughed heartily and I clung on to his belt.

"I am listening as well as I can, for this 'Jan' of yours is like a canoe in storm waves."

Dirk paid no attention to me but went on: "You know the brave Young Hawk? He has the curiosity of a cat and he will steal like a village cur. Well, the captain of this Great Canoe gave food to the delegation and Young Hawk——"

Again Dirk laughed but I did not see anything funny about food. These Broad Breeches are strange in their ways.

"There was on the table a certain small dish and Young Hawk at once dipped his spoon into it and heaped up his plate before the other Mohawks could. Then he took a big spoonful and he stopped eating. Oh! he stopped. And he tried not to show the agony within him. But his tears betrayed him to everybody. Young Hawk pushed the dish, away and he said to the captain: 'The yellow porridge of the Broad Breeches has much strength.'"

Dirk laughed loudly.

I said politely: "I have not eaten the yellow porridge of the Broad Breeches, but when I was at the Great Village on the Rock, the French gave us a taste of a food that was yellow colored. Never have I eaten food of such strength! Was this the yellow porridge that Young Hawk ate?"

"If the French called their dish mustard, it was. Young Hawk ate no more of the captain's food and——"

Dirk shook so I could not hear further.

I did not see why he laughed, and then I remembered about my other father and I asked: "I do not care what Young Hawk eats. I would prefer he fed on poison. He is cruel, like the limping Birch Bark and all Mohawks. But where is my Blackrobe now?"

"After the delegation of Mohawks went away unsuccessful, some of our Dutch feared the Indians would burn and murder if the Blackrobe was let sail away, so when Father Jogues learnt this, he came ashore himself and now is hidden. I will show you where."

We rode in silence for a long time, while I thought over these tidings. Then the Broad Breeches suddenly spoke: "The day before yesterday when I brought Father Jogues some maize I told him I was going with the traders to Ossernenon and he said, if I had the opportunity, to tell you to come to him. Then when I saw the savages were to have another burning tonight, I stayed back. My father thinks I went on ahead of him to Fort Orange, but what I did was to ride ahead and then hide Jan in that thicket. It was quite easy after dark to slip into the village and avoid the Mohawks. I met—— What's that?"

A long howl had risen on the night air. We both looked behind and there onto the edge of the moonlit plain we were two-thirds across came three lean shadows, one after another. A fourth came out of the farther woods and a fifth as I watched.

Dirk dug his moccasined heels into "Jan." We did not speak. There was no need. I thought of those screams of that strange Mohawk I had heard that black night in deer time. This thought made me say a prayer to the Squaw in Blue.

114

League after league we galloped through that brilliant night and the pack kept coming on at an increasing pace.

When the leader was too close behind I took Dirk's bow and twice I fired an arrow that missed. But the third one lodged in the leader and he dropped. Instantly he was buried under a snarling pack. We gained many paces that time.

The horse "Jan" was wild with fright and he galloped till his breath came in long gasps. The pack was after us again.

Jan clattered down the stones of a ford across another stream. Dirk and I leapt off and guided him. In midstream we had to swim. It is easy to swim swiftly when there are wolves on your trail. I, Tarcisius Tandihetsi, say so.

The pack came silently down the stones. Dirk lost his hold on the bridle, for the current was stronger here. I saw him swept downstream. But I had all I could do to hold "Jan's" bridle.

Then Dirk doubled and yelled. The cold water had cramped him. I let go of the maddened animal and struck out after Dirk. His head came up. He gasped and disappeared again. I dove like an otter and caught hold of his breeches. I struck out for the shore. When my feet touched I got a better hold. Dragging Dirk's limp body I struggled up into the branches of a tree. Dirk helped himself very feebly.

"Jan" had crossed the stream. In the shadows I heard his sharp hoofs strike the shore pebbles.

Dirk was coughing up water. But he was able to help himself now and together we climbed higher into the branches of that tree.

Down the moonlit trail towards us came the crazed horse and as we watched, a shadow leapt at his flank and did not let go.

There was a scream and the horse plunged. Almost beneath us his head lifted in agony. More shadows bounded forward and leapt at the animal's throat. . . .

Dirk and I hastily climbed higher.

The Broad Breeches boy was blubbering when he looked down and saw just "Jan's" legs kicking as though he was prancing. The rest of him was hidden under snarling shadows.

"Faithful 'Jan'," Dirk sobbed; "he was only three years old and I raised him from a colt."

A fight had started among two of the leaders and they rose on their hind legs with reeking jaws before they closed in.

The bow and remaining arrows had fallen at the foot of the tree. While Dirk De Witte lay out on an overhanging branch with our two knives ready to hurl at any wolf, I dropped silently to the ground and recovered our weapons.

The wolves were too busy with the carcass to notice us.

When we were safely back in the higher branches, I fitted an arrow. Taking long aim, I let drive at the big leader who had leapt at "Jan's" flank. It was good to see that arrow bury its head in the heart of one wolf.

I had one arrow left. Dirk begged me to let him shoot it, but he agreed with what I said: "Why risk a failure? It will be surer to let me kill another."

So I said a Hail Mary to the Squaw in Blue to help my aim. And she did.

But after that we had to lie there in the tree and watch the six remaining wolves eat their fill.

The moon waned and it was very dark. Below us we could hear the growls of the feeding wolves and sometimes see the darker shadows as they passed underneath our tree to drink from the stream.

Neither Dirk nor I slept, but it was not because of the cold.

Then it was lighter in the east and with the coming of the dawn, the six slunk away.

We waited till the sun was up before we slipped down to the ground, recovered our arrows, and resumed our way towards Fort Orange.

About noontime we met with several servants of Dirk's father. They were mounted. They put us up behind them.

When we came within sight of the fort at the Broad Breeches settlement, Dirk told the servants to put us down. We turned into the forest and soon Dirk led me to the opening of a small cave.

"Stay here. There may be Mohawks in at the post store and if they don't see you, Little Spoon, they will not be able to carry any tales back to Ossernenon and your gentle masters."

This place was very agreeable to me and, though I was hungry, I soon fell asleep, thinking the pleasant thought that Dirk would come shortly and lead me to my other father.

It was very good to think that I was going to see him after all these months among the Mohawk Iroquois. I do not like the Mohawks. I think I prefer the gray wolves. I, Tarcisius Tandihetsi, say so.

Chapter Nineteen

In the Trader's Garret

IT WAS NIGHT when I heard an owl hoot three times and then twice. A minute later Dirk De Witte came up to the entrance of my cave. He had food and while I ate he talked.

A delegation of Iroquois captains of Ossernenon had come to Fort Orange that afternoon and they had demanded the return of Blackrobe. Snake Tooth, Kicking Bear and Partridge were among these captains.

"Do they know where he is?" I asked anxiously.

"No; they do not exactly, but they know he was hidden on the *Wilhelmina*, the Great Canoe in the river, and that he did not sail on her. I told you some of the settlers objected to the Commandant that the Mohawks might raid their farms in their anger if Blackrobe was let sail away. So Father Jogues came ashore of his own accord and the Commandant had him lodged in the house of——"

Dirk broke off and added slyly: "If Little Spoon does not know names he cannot tell names."

"That is very true. But I have finished the food and it is quite dark."

So the Broad Breeches boy led me towards the fort. We entered through a small opening in the stockade that seemed to be very familiar to Dirk. I did not say anything but I am sure I could find that passage again by myself. But I knew Dirk De Witte trusted me and I am a Christian and would not betray him to Iroquois dogs.

118

A sentry challenged, but Dirk called something in his language and the sentry laughed.

Then I was led to a long lodge built after the fashion of these Broad Breeches. It was very wide and substantial, like the breeches they wear.

Dirk opened a door that was unlatched and I heard men breathing heavily. When the Mohawks drink even a little of the strong waters the traders give them, they sleep, breathing heavily. Overhead, I heard men talking.

It was not necessary for Dirk to warn me to tread lightly. That is the only way a Huron ever walks.

A large white cat came into the room. It brushed against Dirk's legs, but when it saw me, it arched its back and it spit at me in a lynx fashion.

"Down, Piet. Down, Piet," ordered the boy. But the cat continued to wave its swollen tail and speak angrily at me.

Dirk had to lift it and dump it outdoors. When he came back, he whispered: "Piet is like all settler's cats. He hates Mohawks worse than dogs."

"But I am no Mohawk." Now I was angry.

The Broad Breeches laughed softly. "Piet does not know the difference between a Huron and an Iroquois."

I was sorry to learn this, for I do not dislike cats, especially when they are cubs.

We walked to a ladder that led up into a black upper room.

Dirk told me: "I must go now. There is one in that garret who expects you. Stay with him till I come again. It is not safe to show yourself, for Partridge, Curly Dog, and other painted friends of yours are nearby."

I started to whisper they were not my friends, but the Broad Breeches faded into the darkness and I heard him calling Piet at the doorway.

I mounted the rough ladder. I felt with my hand but here was

119

no trap door. As soon as my head came through the opening, I saw that a light streamed brokenly between many cracks and chinks in a partition in the middle of the great garret.

Broad Breeches and Mohawks were talking and playing where the strong light was. Many Mohawks sang and I made out Partridge's voice. I have heard him sing much better.

I stood there silently at the head of the ladder until I could see the outlines of some casks and many bunches of vegetables that the fat squaws of the Broad Breeches hang in long rows from the rafters of the ceiling.

A rat scurried across one of the long oblongs of light and then it was silent in this darker half of the garret.

Suspiciously I left the ladder and stood in the darkness. There was not a sound nearby. I do not like to go into the long lodges of the Broad Breeches. They are like traps.

A great shout of laughter came from beyond the lighted partition.

As I looked that way, there came a noise of a slight movement from the darkest corner and I wheeled to face it. I wished I had some weapon.

A voice spoke softly: "Move into the light, Dirk."

I knew that voice and gladly obeyed.

Then I heard: "Tarcisius! So you have come!" And I was kneeling by the side of my other father, holding his mangled hands.

The stumps of his fingers caressed me and I felt as though I was in the bark chapel, back in my village of Teanaustayae, far away in Huronia.

We talked in whispers, sitting there in the deeper shadows that two casks cast.

I told my Blackrobe all the things that had happened to me the many moons I had been separated from him. I told him the good things and the bad things I had done. The worst bad thing was my black thoughts about Wild Berries when we fought in the snow at deer time. When I had finished, my other father said: "For those good deeds He Who knows all things will reward you. And for the other things, well, my Tarcisius is sorry, isn't he?"

I nodded.

"Then make your Act of Contrition and I will give you Absolution and my little one will resolve again to keep that robe of grace he received at the time of Saving Waters spotless and white."

My eyes were accustomed to the darkness now and I could see Blackrobe's mutilated right hand rise and fall and cross the beam of light from beyond the partition, where the Broad Breeches and Mohawks were singing.

I felt very happy and holy within my breast again. It is not so easy to keep good among the cruel pagans.

When I told this to my other father, he said: "I have learnt during this captivity that Our Lord is nearer us here in the country of the Iroquois, where we seemed abandoned than He ever was back across the Great Sea. God is far more powerful to protect those who for His Glory have thrown themselves into the Arms of His Providence than men are wicked to hurt them. Always remember this, Tarcisius. You cannot get beyond the Eye of God nor apart from His Hand."

Then I asked Blackrobe if it were true what Dirk De Witte had told me.

"What has that young Dutchman been telling you?"

"That you had the opportunity to escape down this river to the Broad Breeches' village of New Amsterdam and across the Great Seas to your own country."

"My own country!" exclaimed Blackrobe. "This is my own country, this dear land of my crosses."

His mangled hands swept out into the light and made a wide circle.

"My own country is right here. I love every hill and stream of this land of the Iroquois. I have prayed the Father of Light long and earnestly during these months of captivity to know what is His Will and now it seems to me that it would be better for me to go away for a while that I may return later to gather richer fruit.

"My brothers, the Iroquois, are angry against me because of wars to the north and the loss of some of their braves in battle. If they can obtain my return to Ossernenon just now in the heat of their anger, I would go to God quicker than your father, Eustace, went last year, or as the blessed soul, René Goupil, won his palm at our feet. But I do not feel that my time is come yet. And it will not come before God's own good time. So I have resolved to escape now. I go, but I shall return."

"You will take me with you?" I asked eagerly.

"Why, of course. Did you think I encouraged Dirk to risk his liberty just to leave you here? You shall come with me and later I shall return you to Huronia and your father's squaw, Catherine, if she yet lives."

"That, other father, will fill my breast with joy. But when you come back to the country of the Iroquois I want to come with you as René Goupil did to serve your Mass. I, Tarcisius Tandihetsi, say so."

"I fear that I shall never have the privilege of saying Mass again, my Tarcisius."

Here Blackrobe held up in the shaft of light his mangled hands.

"My brothers, the Iroquois, in their ignorance have made it impossible for this poor priest ever to offer His Lord and Master again."

I knew that my other father was sad within his breast and so I took his mangled hands in mine and I kissed them. And there came over me a feeling. I do not know how to describe it. I forgot this dark garret with its dangers of discovery every moment. I forgot that my other father was an escaped captive and the Mohawk Iroquois would burn him if they recovered him. I forgot also that I was a slave boy, escaped from his master. I knew only the days Saving Waters fell on my head and I made my First Communion had I felt the same. It was as though I was holding, not the mangled hands of a man, but God's Hands were in mine and I was a better boy just to touch them. I, Tarcisius Tandihetsi, say so. . . .

Dirk came before the dawn. I did not wish to leave the trader's garret, but the Broad Breeches boy said: "It is dangerous enough to hide Blackrobe here. My father would not allow you to stay. You must wait in the cave."

So he gave me a bundle of food and dismissed me beyond the stockade.

I said: "You need not tell me where Blackrobe is hidden. I know your father's long lodge."

"Then keep your mouth shut tight on that knowledge, or all of us will be tomahawked by the greased devils of Ossernenon.

"Stay close to the cave. When it is time to go on the Great Canoe with White Wings I will come and get you."

So I started towards the cave and I wish that I had not done so. For as I entered the dark mouth a figure leapt on me and I was struggling in the arms of Wild Berries.

Then I was hit on the head and when I came to I found my arms and legs bound tight with deer thongs and Curly Dog was kicking me.

Curly Dog questioned me, but I would not speak. Finally, he loosened my leg thongs, and I was driven to the place where the delegation of captains from Ossernenon were camped.

Partridge questioned me. I told him, what was the truth, that I had come with the trader's son to see the Broad Breeches' post.

Later that day I was led into Fort Orange with the delegation. White braves with arquebuses herded us to the upper trade room of the trader's long lodge and I heard the Mohawks again demand the return of Blackrobe.

I did not dare to look towards the partition lest I would betray my other father, who lay hidden beyond those rough boards.

It made me glad within my breast to hear the Commandant say: "Ondesonk whom you are seeking, is under my protection. I cannot give him up. You esteem the Dutch enough to yield to our wishes, but to give you full satisfaction, here is gold for the ransom of your prisoner."

The leader of the Broad Breeches held out a pouch and he counted out on the ground a hundred gold pieces, three times.

The Iroquois captains consulted together and finally they took the ransom money. Then they had strong waters that made them happy within and they danced and shouted till the Broad Breeches' servants drove them all out at night time. And Piet, that large white cat of Dirk's, spit at us as we passed through the gates of the fort.

But though the captains had drunk much strong waters, Partridge and Curly Dog kept strict watch on me. Wild Berries too kept watching me. I thought he looked at me the way Piet did.

It was a week later, when Dirk De Witte came into Ossernenon with the traders, who wished to trade back beads and iron pots for those gold pieces, that I had a chance to talk with him. Then I learnt that my other father had sailed on the Great Canoe with the White Wings down the River of the Naked Bear.

I was glad he had escaped and I treasured in my breast that last night in the trader's garret and his promise to return to his poor wretched Huron captives. Blackrobe had said it and I knew Blackrobe did not carry a split tongue, as Partridge did, and the other Mohawks.

This was a memory that I needed in the many sad days of my captivity that were ahead of me. I, Tarcisius Tandihetsi, say so.

Chapter Twenty

The Return of Ondesonk

IT WAS MANY moons later. It was in the beginning of the third summer after my other father had escaped from the cruel Mohawks that I was made glad again. All those times Who Has the Face Black and her family kept me working as their slave. A slave of the Mohawk Iroquois does not know that the sun shines overhead. I, Tarcisius Tandihetsi, a chief's son, say so.

When I felt very sad within my breast I would go to the trees in the woods where Blackrobe had carved the names "Mary" and "Jesus." After I gazed on these marks for a while I did not feel so sad within my breast.

Always I had watched my chance to flee into the dark forests and follow the long trail into the north, back to the villages of my own tribe. Curly Dog read the thoughts of my home that were in my mind and twice he made me watch while escaped captives, my fellow Hurons, were brought back. It was not nice to watch the tortures they had to endure in the long lodge through the black hours of the night, while the braves and squaws and children of the village of Ossernenon cut and bored and broiled the fugitives. When the mercy of the gray dawn came and the brave hearts of the bound captives were stopped with a knife thrust, I rejoiced.

Thus did Charles Tsondatsaa, my father's squaw's brother, go to God in the second summer.

But I learnt the lesson my master intended, and I did not

125

attempt to make my escape. For the Mohawks have eyes in the woods. I think Wild Berries was the eye that gazed on me always.

So it happened that when fishing time came again, and the village sent men to net and trap at Beaver Dam on the upper reaches of the River of the Naked Bear, Who Has the Face Black called me and said: "Little Spoon, take the nets and go with Wild Berries and the others. Wild Berries is your master till you return to Ossernenon."

I saw the cruel lights that lit up in the Iroquois boy's eyes when he learnt that his father's squaw had made me his slave for this fishing trip. I knew there were pains and labors for me. It is never nice to be a captive, and worse to be subject to one who hates you. But I had helps that Wild Berries did not know. I had helps that my Blackrobe had taught me, so I prayed to the Squaw in Blue and, as she always does, she took pity on her poor Huron boy. After that the bundle on my back was lighter as we went down the hillside from the thick palisades of Ossernenon and paddled down the winding River of the Mohawks.

I had another reason to be happier, for it was over eleven moons since I had met the Broad Breeches boy, who was always my friend, and I hoped that Dirk De Witte might be near Beaver Dam. For I knew the custom of the white braves. At fishing time they always went there on horseback with their packs. They traded knives, awls, glass beads, powder and shot for the thunder-sticks for the Iroquois' pelts of beaver, fox, otter, elk, moose, and deer.

I was right, for we had been fishing for less than a week, when the Broad Breeches and their packs arrived.

My lot always was to do squaw's work. At night time I would sit in the stern and paddle, while Wild Berries, standing behind the light of the bark torch in the bows of the canoe with his spear would catch the foolish fish that came up to the light. Then during the days I would help draw in the nets when the fishermen and squaws told me. It is very hard to pull and pull on the long lines when you do not have the time to sleep much at night. Wild Berries would jab me with a cruel stick. He delighted to take his position behind me and with the patience of a lynx he would wait and wait till he thought he caught me resting. Then the jab and always he was courteous, as the Mohawk braves are to the victim when he is bound to the stake and the slow fires are lit.

Wild Berries would say: "My little brother is tired. Let me wake him, lest he sleep. Pull, Little Spoon, pull."

Then he would jab me again with his sharp stick. And I, a captive of his people, must endure in silence.

But I found out by accident a way to make Wild Berries puzzled. Most of the slaves would look sullen, but I learnt to grin at him when the pain was most severe.

This afternoon we had been toiling for hot hours and it was harder to grin at Wild Berries. I was wishing in my heart that God would come and take me, as Blackrobe said He surely would when it was His time.

I was standing up to my waist in the waters, when I heard horsemen at the ford upstream. And there rode up a small party of Broad Breeches.

As they passed us, one of the party looked sharply at me. Then he leapt down from his white horse and shouted at me: "Little Spoon, come ashore."

I recognized Dirk De Witte, grown much taller. I looked to Wild Berries and he refused permission with his head.

When the Broad Breeches boy saw Wild Berries' action he opened his pouch and drawing out a small chain of purple porcelain beads, handed it to the Mohawk, saying: "A present to soothe the master for the loss of his worthless slave's time."

Wild Berries gladly accepted the beads and let me wade ashore.

Dirk laughed when he saw I was ashamed. It is not pleasant even for a captive to be humiliated before another boy. But his laugh was not at me but to make me forget my lost face.

"You will laugh too, Little Spoon, when you hear what I say."

I listened and he told me the news that made me forget my lot.

"Father Jogues, your greatest friend, after he sailed from out of the port of New Amsterdam, did a foolish thing."

"Broad Breeches, you have no sense," I told him gravely. "Nothing Blackrobe does is foolish."

"I know that, for I have liked him ever since the day I first saw him, a livid victim with you in the castles of these painted demons."

Dirk pointed his thumb in the direction of Wild Berries and the other Iroquois fisherfolk, who had crowded around the Broad Breeches traders, eager to barter.

"Yet Father Jogues did a foolish thing." With his eyes that were blue as porcelain beads, he teased me to question him.

"What was the most wise thing my other father did?"

Dirk shook his head. "After getting safely back to France, he only stayed long enough to heal up his wounds, and now word comes to the Commandant of our Fort Orange, that Father Jogues has recrossed the Great Lake and is back in New France."

"That was not foolish. That was like my other father. He loves us Hurons. He is unhappy away from us."

Dirk still teased. "But Father Jogues has done a more foolish thing."

"Tarcisius listens with both ears," I told the smiling Broad Breeches.

"Then Tarcisius will learn the foolishness of the Domine. You know the recent treaty the French and the Iroquois have concluded? We Dutch know it and we know how much to trust the word and the presents of a Mohawk. As much as my father would trust his arquebus to a drunken sentry. Well, the French are sending an embassy to the castles of the Iroquois and one of the Ambassadors is Father Jogues."

I did not at first understand and I questioned anxiously: "My other father is coming back to the village that mangled his hands and tortured him so cruelly! Your tongue, Dirk, is not split like Partridge's, when you speak with me?"

"My tongue is one and whole. Even now the French Ambassadors are due, so I heard Domine John Megapolensis, our good man, say this very morning. One of our runners, a River Indian, has brought word that the party is now beyond this side of the sheet of water you call Where the Lake Closes."

"That is Andiatarocte, where I was with my mistress at eel time last summer. Then I may see my other father before the sun comes again!"

It was very pleasant to think over that thought and I only half listened to Dirk's further words.

But Wild Berries called out that he wanted another present if the Broad Breeches wished to speak longer with "the Huron puppy."

"Dirk, do not waste your beads on the Captain of the Dogs," I told the trader's son, and we grinned at Wild Berries.

Dirk rode back to where his father's servants were busy bartering.

The words he told me were true words, for the next morning the party of Ambassadors came to our place at Beaver Dam.

I stopped gathering wood for the squaw's fires and watched them eagerly. There were about six Mohawk chiefs, whom I did not know, and several whom I recognized as Algonquins, but my eyes were all for the two Frenchmen. One wore a shirt of white linen with a neckband of lace and over all a scarlet cloak. He looked handsome as a cock. But the other was dressed in a poor suit. He was my other father and I would have run and thrown myself at his knees, were Wild Berries not watching me.

He grinned at me and ordered: "Take the canoe and go at once, little brother, to the other bank and there cut me out a new paddle. I have said it."

He called after me: "Cut slowly and do not return from the other bank till I call you. If you finish one paddle, cut another for Curly Dog."

I would gladly have cut the paddle out of his thigh. But the sight of my Blackrobe made me cast out that pagan thought. I could not carry the Devil in my breast when my other father was near.

When Wild Berries called me back it was towards evening. The Ambassadors and their party had gone on to Fort Orange.

Wild Berries mocked me, seeing the paddles. "Most excellently done, little brother."

He took the paddles and smashed them with a tomahawk. "I'll let you make another tomorrow when the fishing nets are in."

It was very hard to grin at him, but I managed. He continued: "I know it will please you to hear that Ondesonk knew me and inquired for you. I told him that you came and begged me to let you hide yourself in the woods till he had gone."

I told the Mohawk boy: "Blackrobe knows that your mouth is too large. The words come from it too easily."

Wild Berries did not understand, so I explained most gladly: "Blackrobe is most wise. He knows always on one side of your face you see clearly; on the other side it is striped so your sight is not good. The painted side is towards us Hurons. You do not see a bit there. The clean side is towards your tribe. Blackrobe sees that as clear as noon. And the captives of my tribe in Ossernenon will tell him about me."

Wild Berries slunk away without another word.

But he would have kept me hauling fishnets till my other father had returned to Canada if he had his way.

As it was, Who Has the Face Black sent for me and I arrived back at Ossernenon after the presents had been exchanged and the peace council was over.

I learnt that Blackrobe had brought handsome presents of beaver skins and arm lengths of porcelain, three fingers wide, from Onontio, the French Commander of the lands along the Great River. These gifts the Mohawk chiefs accepted and promised to keep the peace. But I did not believe their words; no captive did.

I sought in the village and Jumping Rabbit told me where Blackrobe was. So I went to the long lodge of Who Keeps the Kettle, the ancient squaw Blackrobe used to call his aunt.

And there after all these moons I was able to fall at the feet of my other father and weep for joy.

With his mangled hands he soothed me and made me feel good within again, like the little boy I had been in far away Teanaustayae.

Many things he told me of his trip across the Great Lake and how the white people of his tribe made him ashamed with their honors. Then I learnt that William Couture had escaped from Tionnontoguen, and likewise Bernard Atieronhonk, my cousin, and both were at the Great Village on the Rock.

Long into the black night I lay at his feet and listened to my other father telling these tales and the news that the canoe parties of Hurons, who annually came down the Great River, brought of my people in Huronia. I learnt about my father's squaw, Catherine, and my brothers and sisters.

While Blackrobe talked with us captives, he let me hold his mangled hands. It made me forget those sad months away from him to do so. I, Tarcisius Tandihetsi, say so.

Chapter Twenty-One

The Buried Mass Box

THE AMBASSADORS, who came with Onontio's gifts to confirm the peace, had a special long lodge. Here early next morning all the Christian Hurons who had heard that the Prayer had come back to Ossernenon, met.

Blackrobe heard our sins and he raised his right hand and forgave them as God had given him the power to do. When their turn came I saw two Hurons take out a little bundle of sticks that they kept to remember their sins by, and look at them one by one. Then they told the bad things they had done during these many moons Blackrobe had been away.

When all were pardoned my other father said to me: "Tarcisius, has my former altar boy completely forgotten his responses at Holy Mass?"

I had to tell him that there were some of the longer ones I did not remember. But my other father took me aside and he recalled to my mind the altar-boy words I had learnt to say in our little bark chapel back in those pleasant days when Blackrobe said his Mass and I served him. It seemed so long ago.

I looked down at his mangled hands and when he saw me doing this, he told me: "Though I am unworthy, yet while I was across the Great Lake, the Great Father, who is God's Captain on earth, heard of my mutilations and in his kindness he granted me permission again to offer the Holy Mass with these."

Here Blackrobe held up his maimed fingers. Though he did

not tell me so, yet I have since heard that the Great Father wept when he gave the permission and he said the noble words, "It would be unjust that a martyr of Christ should not drink the Blood of Christ." I think the Great Father spoke true words about my Blackrobe. And I would tell the Great Father this, if I met him. I, Tarcisius Tandihetsi, say so.

All of the captive Christians knelt about the lodge that the Ambassadors had and now the squaw, Theresa, and an Algonquin squaw set up a table and over it hung two beautiful elk robe skins that Who Keeps the Kettle lent them.

Then the Frenchman who was the fellow Ambassador of Blackrobe, opened one of the bundles and there were Mass gowns and candles and Book.

When Blackrobe was vested and the candles lit, he took the small chalice under the veil and placing his mangled hands on top of it, he nodded to me.

All were kneeling back and around the table. Some of the squaws were weeping. They were very happy. Pagan Mohawks scowled in the dim smoky background, but as Blackrobe had come as an Ambassador from Onontio and their sachems had taken gifts of porcelain belts, they did not dare stop him.

I answered what I remembered, and the white brave, who was the other Ambassador, supplied what I forgot. But all the time, while my other father said Holy Mass, I kept repeating, "Jesus, have pity on me." I wished to prepare my heart to receive Him when the time came. For the last time God came into my heart was the Feast of St. Ignatius, the first Blackrobe, a few days before Snake Tooth's war party took us captives.

Once I looked beyond the robe-hung compartment of the long lodge and there was Wild Berries watching me. I saw that he was jealous. I knew he was thinking I helped the Christian medicine man at his rites. Wild Berries is very superstitious. But he is a pagan. All pagans are superstitious. I used to be when I was Little Spoon, and carried the Devil in my breast all the day.

When the time came Blackrobe spoke the words that brought God down on the altar. I looked up as he lifted the Host high in his mangled hands. I said again, "Jesus, have pity on me."

Then I did not think of the years of hard life I had as a slave in the castles of our enemies. I felt my heart grow soft with love for Blackrobe, who had come back the long trail to the land of his crosses. For such my other father called this country of the Mohawk Iroquois. What would we have done, if Blackrobe had not returned to us? So I prayed God hidden there on the altar to make all things good for my other father.

I could see that Blackrobe had forgotten us who knelt about him there in the smoky long lodge. He seemed to see God in the Host he held in his mangled hands and for a long time he talked with Him. I knew he was asking good things for us.

Then it was the time when God would come to me and I told Him how sorry I was for all the bad things I had done since Saving Waters fell on my head.

First of all the Christians, Blackrobe gave me God. This is an altar boy's privilege. I did not remember that I was a slave here in Ossernenon. I felt good as I had been the morning when my other father first gave me God, back in my own village of Teanaustayae. I cried and I did not care if Wild Berries and Jumping Rabbit and the other Mohawk boys were grinning in the smoky background. They are pagans and they did not know. I would have minded if they had seen my tears when I was tortured, but I did not care if they did now.

When Holy Mass was over and Blackrobe had finished his priest prayers, he called me to his side and told me sad news.

"Tarcisius, I have failed. Your mistress, Who Has the Face Black, will not accept a ransom belt for you. I have offered her three thousand beads. She refuses. So, son of mine, I must go today and leave you here among our brothers, the Iroquois."

Blackrobe saw by my face what I did not try to hide from his gaze.

"I know how deep is your disappointment. All the time of the council I have tried to make Who Has the Face Black accept your ransom, but they know the custom. She is not obliged and the chiefs of the village will not force her."

"I will run away," I told him angrily.

"It's a long trail into the north and few fugitives arrive at the bank of the Saint Lawrence. William Couture suffered terrible things on the trail. He was almost recaptured twice."

My other father did not need to tell me what happened to those captives who fled and were brought back to the village fires. I had seen them die. It was not good.

Said Blackrobe: "Partridge and my good aunt have warned me that, now the council is over, it will be better to hasten our departure."

"I know why!" I cried.

"Why, Tarcisius?"

"Because I overheard two chiefs and they said a band of Iroquois from the other castles are already on the war path. They are out to lie in ambush for my countrymen coming down the Great River."

"This I have heard also, and that is why John Bourdon and I have decided to return without visiting Andagaron and Tionnontoguen and consoling the captives there."

My other father looked sad when he said this to me. Then his brown eyes lighted and he promised: "But be of good heart, Tarcisius, and tell your fellow captives that Ondesonk returns to Onontio to report as his Ambassador. Yet he will come again into this dear land ere the snow comes thickly and he will remain with his Huron children till Spring. Tell this in all the villages. I have given presents of wampum and they have been received. I shall return shortly. Now, is not that good news that will cheer up my Tarcisius?"

I nodded sadly, for now that my other father was back in Ossernenon, I did not wish to see him leave. I knew while my mistress refused the ransom beads I must stay here. That was a selfish thought and I put it away.

"There is a young white brave a few years older than you at Quebec," Blackrobe now told me. "He crossed the Great Lake lately. He is eager to work for God. And if my Superiors grant permission, he will be my altar boy when I return. You will like him, for I have often told him about you."

"What is his name?"

"The lad is Jack Lalande. You will like him."

"If my other father likes him, then so must I," I answered politely.

"Ah, Little Spoon! Little Spoon! I saw a green light glow in your eyes then."

I did not think that this was possible, for my eyes are black as night, but I know Blackrobe had seen that I was jealous of this other altar boy. I hung my head and my other father put his mangled hands on my bare shoulders and said in kindly tones: "Little chickens fear the kite, little lambs run from the wolves, and little savages abhor any restraint on their hearts. Do not be a little savage, little son of God."

I whispered: "Other father, I will pray that I may see this Jack Lalande.". . .

At noon Blackrobe called some of the village chiefs into the long lodge and there he opened the small box in which he kept his Mass gowns and supplies. Carefully he showed each article to the circle of silent, smoking Iroquois.

He explained: "These I am leaving in this box. For after I report to Onontio in the Great Village on the Rock, that the Iroquois have thrown away the tomahawk and the French have spilled the powder for their arquebuses on the ground I will come back to your castle, not as Onontio's Ambassador, but as a Blackrobe to tell you the Prayer."

The Iroquois listened in silence. I knew that some, especially of the Bear clan, did not want Blackrobe to come back. I think my other father knew that, though he never showed by any sign that he thought the Prayer was not welcome.

Blackrobe looked around the circle and called out: "Where, chiefs of Ossernenon, shall I leave this box?"

Partridge spoke up: "Ondesonk, we see what is in that box. You have shown us all. But we know not all. Maybe, it is not good medicine. Therefore, I believe the box should be put under ground."

All the chiefs grunted their approval of this plan.

"Then show me where I shall bury it and that I will do," offered Blackrobe.

Silently Partridge and Kicking Bear got up. I picked up the box and, followed by Blackrobe and a crowd, we went to his aunt's compartment.

Here Partridge pointed to the ground. The squaws dug swiftly. While the Iroquois in the long lodge watched, Blackrobe had me put the box in the hole and his aunt, Who Keeps the Kettle, piled up and tapped down the earth over the cover.

If I had only known at the time what my other father was doing, I would have prevented him with my life.

That afternoon I kissed my other father's mangled hands and he blessed me, whispering: "I go, but I shall return to my good Tarcisius before the snow is on the ground. Now, little son of mine, stand fast in the Prayer wherever you go. Remember the example of the Roman boy whose name you received when I poured Saving Waters on your brow. Whatever may happen, Tarcisius, trust in the Good God and keep yourself pure and brave in the midst of pagans as your namesake did. This I pray for you always, Tarcisius. And may God reunite us in His Holy Paradise if it should chance we do not see each other again here below."

I nodded and then, to show him I was no longer jealous, I whispered: "I will be good to this other boy, Jack Lalande, when you return."

Then I stopped for I did not trust myself to speak, and I went away.

I watched from the gate of the palisades the Ambassadors and their party go down the hillside and cross the flats and the ford and take the long trail that led to the Great River.

I did not feel good. Who Has the Face Black treated me more kindly after that. She did not let Wild Berries have charge of me. I think my Blackrobe must have given my mistress a handsome present to make her heart soft towards me. It would be like my other father to think to do so, when he failed to ransom me.

But all that summer, when I toiled as a slave of the Iroquois toils in the fields of corn, hoeing and harvesting, I remembered that first Holy Mass in Ossernenon, when God came into my heart again to make me strong. I counted the days till the nuts would begin to fall, for I knew Blackrobe, if he was alive, would keep his word. His tongue is not split and he would return to the country of the Mohawk Iroquois. And I was right. I, Tarcisius Tandihetsi, say so.

Chapter Twenty-Two

Evil Spirits Rise

THAT SEASON before the nuts began to fall, many signs were about that the Mohawk Iroquois would have an evil winter and that there would be many empty bellies in Ossernenon. The first trouble came when the corn in the fields beyond the palisades did not rise above my head, for many worms devoured leaf and stalk. We captives toiled and the squaws toiled but the worms won and when the time came there was little corn to gather.

The pagans sorcerers went to the fields and they danced and shook their tortoise-shell rattles. They beat their drums for hours. They called on Sun, their bad god. And they fell down exhausted. But the corn did not grow tall. I who saw these ceremonies knew that it would not, for He Who gives all things, was not pleased with these superstitions.

This I told to my mistress, Who Has the Face Black, when she was making a moccasin for Wild Berries. She said: "I would that Ondesonk was still with us. He had very powerful medicine. He was different from our sorcerers. He lived a good life and his tongue was not split."

When I heard her say these things, I was glad within my breast. For before, she had beaten Who Keeps the Kettle, whom my other father called his aunt, when that squaw spoke words in praise of Blackrobe.

Eagerly I told my mistress of Blackrobe's promise to return and spend the winter in Ossernenon.

139

Wild Berries, who had been listening, lying on some fur pelts in the corner of our compartment of the long lodge, here spoke up: "You both speak with a split tongue. I listened at the council of the sachems last night. Partridge and the limping Birch Bark said the worms in the corn are due to the evil spirits that Ondesonk put in the box with his sorcerer's clothes. That box lies buried under the compartment of Who Keeps the Kettle. The whole village knows that. I have spoken."

When Who Has the Face Black heard her son say this lie, she was silent and went on beading the moccasin.

The next afternoon, when I was helping the pottery moulders beyond the palisades, I heard the conch shells blowing from the trail across the River of the Mohawks. But it was not the long sound that told of the return of the warriors laden with captives and booty.

All rushed down the hill from Ossernenon, and at the bottom we saw three braves. The eagle feathers were gone from their hair; dark stains were caked over their blue and red-barred war paint. Two of the braves limped the way Birch Bark does, and only one was able to paddle the canoe across the waters.

When the squaws recognized the warriors, they raised the Song of Mourning. It is very sad to hear them sing it.

Curly Dog was the warrior without wounds. In the center of the village he told how the white braves with powerful arquebuses had ambushed and killed all the rest of the war party on the shore of the Great River. There had been twenty-eight warriors who left Ossernenon. Snake Tooth had led this party and he had not returned, nor did Kicking Bear.

We captives did no work that afternoon, for all the squaws chanted their Song of Mourning and the village curs howled.

About the council fire the older men sat and smoked. I heard one after another rise and each said evil spirits were angry and Sun, their bad god, was angry.

Then the withered old sorcerer, White Oak, got up. When he spoke it was to blame all the troubles that had come to Ossernenon on the magic box with the evil spirits of Ondesonk imprisoned within it.

When he was done, sorcerers danced till I grew dizzy watching them. Then one said: "I know the word that the Broad Breeches who keeps the store at Fort Orange told me. This is it: 'You Iroquois have no sense, listening to the Prayer of Ondesonk. He wishes to pour Saving Waters on the heads of as many Mohawks as possible that when you go to the Heaven of the French, they may burn you at their leisure.'"

Hours and hours of the night they spoke such wicked lies at the council, and none in the village slept that night.

Only one Iroquois voice was raised against this false opinion of the Prayer and that was the voice of Who Keeps the Kettle. She whom my other father called his aunt, demanded that the sachems and sorcerers hear her words.

All listened in silence when the old squaw began: "It is true that Sun is angry with Ossernenon. It is true that evil spirits have sent worms into our corn fields. It is true that the thunder-sticks of the split-tongued white braves have broken the peace and slain our warriors."

Here the squaws whose braves had not come back to the village raised their mournful chant, but Who Keeps the Kettle shouted above the sound of their wailings: "But it is not true that Ondesonk has sent these evils on our village. It is not true. It is not true. He was my captive. This council gave him to me for the son who did not come back from the shores of the Great River. He lived in my long lodge all the moons he was here and I know he is a good man. Ondesonk has only right feelings in his breast for this village and all Iroquois. He would not bury an evil spirit. What the sorcerers say is split-tongued. And the Broad Breeches are split-tongued. They are jealous of Ondesonk and the white men of the

Great River. They fear lest we trade peltries to the French instead of to them. Maybe they implore Sun to send these evils on our village."

More this old squaw would have said, but the sachems would not let her.

Here a cunning sorcerer who was so old that I have heard Who Has the Face Black say he was born before the white men ever came to the countries to the north, got up to speak. He did not belong in Ossernenon and I do not know his name.

He claimed he had had a dream and in it Sun appeared to him with an angry countenance and told him all the truth. That was why he had come to Ossernenon. At this all the Iroquois edged closer, for he spoke without many teeth and it was not easy to hear his words. He claimed that Sun told him Ondesonk had hidden three very powerful evil spirits in the box he had buried. One had killed the corn in the fields; another had made the thunder-sticks of the white braves kill the warriors; and the third would bring the Quick Death into the long lodges of the village.

This ancient sorcerer was listened to very attentively. Even the squaws whose braves had not come back were silent when he was done.

It was towards the hours before the dawn and sleep was in the eyes of all, so the captain of the village gave the signal and the council was over.

But there was no council the next night, for that day Quick Death came within the palisades.

I do not know what manner of death this is. I had never seen its like, but braves and squaws and papooses and slaves came down with high fever and they lay still in nearly all the compartments of the long lodges.

Six of my fellow captives died within three days. Everywhere the sorcerers went and sang and made their wicked signs over the dying, but the Mohawks died; some even as the sorcerers chanted.

As Blackrobe had instructed me, I poured Saving Waters on the foreheads of nine little Iroquois papooses before they went to God.

The fourth night while a council was being held, I went alone to Who Keeps the Kettle's compartment and I dug till I had Blackrobe's Mass box exposed. I opened it and I took out all my other father's things. I put stones within the box and I put it back and stamped down the earth.

I took the Mass things and, wrapping them in a deer skin, I sneaked into the ravine where Blackrobe and I had tried to find René Goupil's body. I hid the Mass things in a hollow tree and I put stones and twigs on top so that no Iroquois and no wolf or fox could get at them.

Then I went to my mat of husks and slept. I felt better.

The next morning a mob came to Who Keeps the Kettle's compartment. The ancient sorcerer, White Oak, was at their head. They knocked down my other father's aunt when she tried to stop them, and they had to hold her, for she talked fast words. The old squaw was not afraid of any in the village, and I think the braves feared her more than a war club. Who Keeps the Kettle had a very sharp tongue. She made some of those she was not talking to laugh very much.

But all the time some of the Mohawks were digging till they had unearthed the small box. When it lay exposed none would touch it through fear of the evil spirits. Then White Oak ordered an Algonquin squaw to pick it up and carry it to the village street.

I knew what they were going to find and I was very glad nobody had seen me last night. Partridge was opening the box, when the old sorcerer, White Oak, warned: "Do not do that! You have no sense, Partridge. You will let more evil spirits out."

Some wanted to burn the box, but again White Oak objected: "Fire cannot hurt the evil spirits that Ondesonk imprisoned in this box. Only water and drowning will hurt them. Tonight let us burn three Huron captives instead."

When he had finished, two squaw captives were made to take up the box and they carried it down the hillside, while the sorcerers chanted wildly.

In a deep spot of the River of the Mohawks they sunk it. And the ancient sorcerer, White Oak, said that Sun was now angry with the village no longer.

This was superstition that only pagans believe in. When I was a pagan I would have believed this too, but I knew no evil spirits would have stayed with the Holy Mass gowns that I had seen Blackrobe place in that box against the day of his return.

I was very sad within my breast as I came up the hill, for I began to fear that now if my other father came back at the beginning of the time when nuts fall, he would not be able to say Holy Mass and give me my God again. He would be burnt quickly. But I felt glad within my breast that I had hidden the Mass things. I knew my Blackrobe would like that. I, Tarcisius Tandihetsi, say so.

Chapter Twenty-Three

The Dream of Wild Berries

THEN CAME the afternoon when Quick Death entered into the long lodge of Who Has the Face Black and it seized her son, Wild Berries. My mistress cried as I had never seen her cry. I felt sorry for her and more sorry for the Mohawk boy. He had done cruel things to me, but then he was a pagan and he did not know any better. I was afraid that he would die and go to the place where the fires burn forever. I prayed to the Squaw in Blue for Wild Berries. I did not want him to go away forever.

Who Has the Face Black went with gifts of long beads and begged the sorcerers to come. I would have gone outside the long lodge, for I did not wish to see the devil things sorcerers do, but my mistress ordered me to stay by. I was a slave and I had to.

An old sorcerer shook his tortoise shell and danced. Then he called for an earthenware vessel of fresh water. Who Has the Face Black went herself to get it. The sorcerer took it and gazed a long time at the water. He shook his head and he looked into the glowing coal fire. These things he did, pretending to see the nature of Wild Berries' sickness. At last he straightened up and, going to the mat on which Wild Berries tossed, he hung on the boy three discs of porcelain quills. And he began to chant to Sun, their bad god, and begged him to take the Quick Death away and make it go into one of the Christian captives of the village.

When this nonsense was over, the sorcerer shook Wild Berries and asked him: "Tell me, my nephew, what did you dream of last night?"

Wild Berries muttered something that I could not hear. But the cunning sorcerer put his ear close to the Mohawk boy's lips and pretended to listen closely.

He stood up and said: "The boy, Wild Berries, says he saw an empty canoe, sailing, sailing away and it had a spear with an arrow pierced through it, planted in the bows. That is a very bad sign."

When Who Has the Face Black heard this, she ordered me to run out and cut a piece of soft wood.

This I did and when I came back there were three sorcerers dancing around Wild Berries. His mat had been moved out of the compartment and now he lay by the fireplace. The sorcerers carried the image of Sun, made of six thousand porcelain beads, that hung in the long lodge of the sachems.

While these sorcerers danced and chanted, Who Has the Face Black took the piece of wood from me and gave it to the old sorcerer. He demanded her sharpest knife and with it he quickly fashioned the rude outline of the dream canoe. In the bows he stuck a little sliver of spear and pierced the spear with a smaller arrow.

Then all the sorcerers sang to Sun, their bad god, and they put their hands on the body of Wild Berries. He struggled and cried to Who Has the Face Black. But the youngest sorcerer held his hands fast over the model of the canoe with the spear and arrow. All three began a bad prayer to Sun and begged him to take this canoe and tie the Quick Death with deer thongs in the bottom of it and make it sail away from the spirit of Wild Berries. And they held Wild Berries till he lay still, exhausted from his struggles. I thought he had died. None of the sorcerers would let me come near him. For I wished to speak with Wild Berries.

Then I remembered René Goupil had liked this boy and I went into a dark corner of the smoky long lodge and kneeling down prayed to that companion of my Blackrobe.

This is what I said: "O René Goupil, ask the Squaw in Blue to beg her Son not to let Wild Berries die without Saving Waters on his forehead. He is a pagan and though he did cruel things to me, I forgive him. I do not want him to burn forever. Blackrobe said you were a Martyr of Christ and martyrs get what they want. Ask the Squaw in Blue for this."

And I said my fingers full of Hail Marys as my other father had taught me to say when I wanted anything from the Squaw in Blue.

I remembered that last day on the Great River, in the canoe with my other father, when he told me about little Isaac and how the Squaw in Blue had walked in the midst of the flames and brought the boy water and food.

Never did I seem to want something as I wanted Saving Waters on the forehead of Wild Berries before the Quick Death made him stiff.

When it grew dark within the long lodge the sorcerers ceased their wicked songs over the Mohawk boy. Who Has the Face Black gave them more beads and they went away. Wild Berries kept tossing about.

Who Has the Face Black never left his side while the night passed. I tried to keep awake but my eyes would not obey and I slept.

The black night must have been half over when Who Has the Face Black woke me, saying: "My son is awake and is calling for you. Go to him, Little Spoon."

Wild Berries lay under the best elk robe his father's squaw owned and he was very weak. But the lights from the coals in the fireplace flickered in his dark eyes and I saw they were very bright.

When I sat at his side he took my hand in his and his hand was hot as a fagot that lies near the fire.

He said: "Listen, Little Spoon, and you listen too, my father's squaw. I have had a dream; such a beautiful dream."

Who Has the Face Black was weeping but she stopped, for always these Mohawk Iroquois listen intently to the story of dreams.

"This is what I dreamt. You remember that white brave, who was Ondesonk's companion, and Birch Bark tomahawked him? This one came before me and with him were many papooses of our village. All had the Sign of the Prayer on their forehead. These Signs were brighter than many fires at night. They were bright as the sun in summer time, and it seemed to hurt my eyes to look."

Wild Berries lifted himself and resting his weight on his arm, continued eagerly: "In the midst of these was a young Squaw. She wore a blue robe. It was very beautiful and must have been worth many, many elk skins. The white brave and the papooses knelt at her feet. She carried in her arms a Papoose. He was more beautiful than any papoose I ever saw. When my eyes were on Him, I forgot to look at the white brave and the Squaw in the Blue Robe. This Papoose in the Squaw's arms looked at me and as He did my heart within my breast became very sweet. The Squaw in the Blue Robe worth many elk skins spoke and she said words that I do not remember.

"But when I woke up there was the desire within my breast to have that Sign on my forehead too."

Wild Berries stopped and I said anxiously: "Listen, Mohawk boy, I will put it there as Ondesonk put it on the papooses in the village. It is the good Sign of the Prayer that Ondesonk uses."

This I told Wild Berries and other things about the Prayer till Who Has the Face Black told me to get water and I ran to do so. I was very glad within my breast.

When I came back I poured Saving Waters on the forehead of Wild Berries, saying the words as my other father had taught me....

Later, the look of those whom Quick Death seizes fast came into the Mohawk's boy's eyes and he muttered many things till he went to God as daylight came.

In the weeks after the Quick Death let go its hold on the long lodges of the village. The sorcerers said it was due to Sun being no longer angry. But that is only superstition.

Though it was late, two large war parties went on the trail to the north. These war bands were very angry with the French for killing Snake Tooth's party and, as the Mohawk custom is, they wanted scalps and captives for the burnings to avenge this defeat.

I had one fear now and that was that Blackrobe would attempt to come back. I wished I could send a message warning him of all that had happened in Ossernenon. Then I thought, perhaps, Dirk De Witte might be able to help me, for I knew he liked my other father. And I watched for the chance to meet him, but that chance did not come for many days, as the Broad Breeches kept away from Ossernenon and they would not let the Mohawks within their stockade at Fort Orange. They feared the Quick Death very much.

Then one afternoon when the nuts were beginning to fall the Broad Breeches boy came riding into Ossernenon with his father, the trader.

When we met, Dirk De Witte listened to all my fears and then he increased them by saying:

"Blackrobe thinks the cantons of the Mohawks are at peace with the French. It is not so and if he attempts to return to this village, they will kill him, especially those of the Bear Clan, for I have heard rumors that some of the young braves of that clan have taken an oath to lie in wait for him. They blame him for all the troubles that have happened to Ossernenon since the day he left here as an Ambassador."

"Cannot you find some way to warn him?" This I asked, though within my breast I knew that this hope was very faint.

"The only way, Little Spoon, I will be able to warn him will be if he escapes the war parties in the north and takes the trail through Fort Orange. I know our Commandant will never let him leave the fort's gates. It would be suicide. I do not see why he wants to return.

He got safely to Europe. He was tortured here and yet he returns. Why does he come back?"

I, who knew Blackrobe's love for his captive Huron children knew the reason, but I felt that Dirk, being white skinned, would not understand, so I held my peace.

But when Dirk De Witte quitted the village the following day, I began a prayer to the Squaw in Blue that she would keep my other father out of all harm. I know she will—and me too. I, Tarcisius Tandihetsi, say so.

Chapter Twenty-Four

October 18, 1646

I WAS DOWN by the bank of the River of the Mohawks helping Curly Dog mend a canoe when I heard the first conch shell blow. The war party was not yet visible. The signals announced they had captives. There would be no more work in the village that day. Soon the party came into view on the northern bank of the river.

Curly Dog made me paddle him across the river in the canoe we were mending. With his foot he held a piece of bark in place over the leak while I paddled.

I could hear the whooping village of Ossernenon coming down the long slope to give their cruel welcome. I felt very sorry for these unknown captives, thinking of the awful afternoon more than four years ago when I was driven up that hillside before my other father.

A dip in the Mohawk trail hid the war party and so I was quite close under the other bank before I made them out. The captives were huddled together and their chief, whom I knew as Young Hawk, was waiting for us as we grounded.

It was only then I heard him tell Curly Dog: "We have Ondesonk and one young white brave who was with him."

I leapt from the canoe and ran up the muddy bottom to the spot under some willows where the captives were guarded.

It was indeed my other father and he had been cruelly tortured on the trail. Two Noses, who guarded him, drove me away. I saw the white brave who was with Blackrobe. He was very young. He could not have been more than two years or three years older than I. His hair was light brown and curly, and though he had suffered also, he did not look sad. There was a smile on his face when Blackrobe spoke to him and nodded towards me. I stood by a willow tree, for I knew Two Noses would throw a knife at me if I, a slave, went closer without his permission.

I heard White Oak, the old sorcerer of the Bear Clan, taunting Blackrobe. He yelled: "You shall die tomorrow, Ondesonk. Do not fear. You shall not be burnt. Your head and your companions' shall fall beneath our tomahawks and we shall set them on the palisades towards the north to show them for many a day to your brethren whom we capture."

Quickly the captives were driven into the canoes that had come and Young Hawk got into the canoe I had paddled. I saw there was an arrow wound in his thigh that had festered, making his whole right leg useless. How he had followed the trail all the leagues from the northern lands by the Great River I do not know. It must have been terrible pain to walk league after league. He must have limped the way Birch Bark does ever since the bear clawed him.

Before I paddled Young Hawk and Curly Dog across the River of the Mohawks, the captives had been landed on the other bank and already whooping Mohawks were lined up in the two narrow lines, leaving a lane between them. The brave and squaws and children were armed with the thorny sticks and the long iron bars that came from the Broad Breeches post. These hurt more than the thorny sticks.

Young Hawk was telling Curly Dog his party had surprised Blackrobe and the Christian Hurons who were with him. They had stalked them for two-days' march, when they found out that Blackrobe was coming back to Ossernenon, and then had ambushed them on the night of the third day. Many of my tribe escaped into the woods.

It was at the very beginning of this attack that Young Hawk had been struck with the arrow. He had tomahawked my countryman who had shot the bow. He pointed to the dried scalp lock hanging at his apron. I kept wondering if I had known that slain chief of my people.

I felt hot within my breast when he went on: "The rest of the trail south I made Ondesonk carry me on his shoulders."

Young Hawk was angry because his wound prevented his following my countrymen who fled into the woods and making captives of all of them. More than fifteen had escaped. They were coming with Blackrobe to visit relatives among the captives in the Mohawk castles.

It must have been easy to waylay Blackrobe's party, for they thought the Iroquois were at peace with the French. They did not know of the pestilence and the breaking of the peace that Blackrobe had made only three months before.

More I did not hear, for we had grounded on the Ossernenon side of the River of the Mohawks.

Curly Dog ordered me to help Young Hawk up the hill, and we slipped twice following the path where the new captives had run the gauntlet.

When we arrived at the top where the stage was erected, it was like the painting of Hell and the Demons, that hangs in the little chapel in my native village of Teanaustayae.

All were abusing my Blackrobe for the troubles that had come on Ossernenon since he was there last.

As I looked, Partridge was cutting a long strip from the flesh on the arm of my other father and he was shouting: "Let us see whether this white flesh is the flesh of a Manitou."

I came close to the stage and I heard Blackrobe replying: "Partridge, my brother, you know that is not so. I am no Manitou. I have no communion with evil spirits. It is your sorcerers who know them. I have brought nothing to this land but the Prayer and my great love for you and your children. Why do you torture a friend?"

White Oak hobbled forward and he shouted: "Ondesonk, you buried evil spirits in that box and they sent the worm into our corn. They sent the Quick Death into our long lodges. They sent disaster on our war parties and our young men do not return to Ossernenon any more."

He was interrupted by an old squaw screaming: "It was your sorcery, Ondesonk, that brought the Quick Death on my son, Full Moon. Ondesonk, you liked your young companion. I will treat him as you treated my son."

And she climbed upon the stage and fell on the young white brave, whom I knew was the other altar boy Blackrobe had called Jack Lalande. She had the stone knife and with it she hacked at his thumb....

I saw Lalande look at Blackrobe, and my other father looked up to the skies.

More I did not see, for Curly Dog ordered me to help Young Hawk into the long lodge, where the sorcerers and the old squaws might treat his thigh with the healing herbs.

I was frightened for Blackrobe. This time I knew he could not escape the stake and the flames.

When the council met in the long lodge of White Oak I was not able to get in. Later, I stopped Jumping Rabbit, who had heard all, and he said: "Ondesonk and the rest of the captives are to die tonight. It is decided. They are already dead dogs."

But this was a lie he told me, because he knew I loved Blackrobe and he was mocking me.

I learnt from the squaw Theresa that the council had decided to spare the lives of my other father and the young white brave. But the five Huron captives were to burn before dawn next morning.

Before the long lodge of Who Has the Face Black I happened to come upon White Oak and Curly Dog. They were talking in high voices and they did not see me.

October 18, 1646

This is what the ancient sorcerer White Oak said: "The Wolf and the Turtle Clans outvoted the Bear, Ondesonk is to live. It is not good. He will teach the Prayer."

Here Curly Dog exclaimed: "There is nothing more repulsive than this Prayer of Ondesonk. It exterminates all that we Mohawks hold dearest."

"Brother, you say true words," replied White Oak, who has a split tongue. "If Ondesonk lives, he will loosen more evil spirits on our village. Sun will be angry. Sun does not wish this. Listen, I will invite him to supper this evening and do you, my nephew, be by the bear skin door when he stoops to enter."

Curly Dog smiled wickedly.

I did not stay to hear more. Already I knew too much.

When I was free from my squaw work I went to the long lodge where my other father was held. On the way I said a prayer to the Squaw in Blue that I might not be stopped. And I was not.

The guard, Two Noses, did not prevent my passage. It was smoking and dim within the long lodge. When my eyes were able to see, I made out Blackrobe, lying on a skin in one of the compartments. His wounds were pitiful, even though his old mistress, Who Keeps the Kettle, had come with herbs and dressings.

I was on my knees beside him and I had his mangled hands in mine. These I kissed repeatedly and I felt peace within my breast.

I spoke speedy words and told my other father all. I begged him not to accept this invitation to supper tonight.

He shook his head. "If the council has spared my life and White Oak and Curly Dog come and invite me, Tarcisius, it would be a mortal insult to refuse them. I will not refuse."

"But, other father, they plan to kill you."

"That is within God's Hands. They cannot harm me before His appointed time. Maybe this is His appointed time."

I saw my other father's face. He looked as if he was seeing very pleasant things. But I saw nothing.

155

"Tell me," he asked after a while, "is Jack Lalande, my young companion, included in this invitation?"

I told Blackrobe that I had not heard that he was.

"Then when I have gone to White Oak's lodge, do you find where they have the lad and tell him this message from me."

"Gladly, I will that."

"Tell him to have courage for a little while longer—such a little time."

I knew then my other father was going to God and tears came quickly to my eyes.

"And may I not go with you? These years of captivity here are so tiresome!"

"Listen, little Tarcisius," begged my other father, "there was a poor priest once who felt that way, and while he was praying before a rude birch-bark tabernacle, he heard a Voice saying distinctly, 'Be courageous and steadfast.' These words have strengthened him down to this blessed hour.

"Nothing is tiresome that is endured for God, little son. That complaint was spoken by the lips of Little Spoon, not by the Christian tongue of my Tarcisius. Be courageous and steadfast, Tarcisius."

Then I was silent and Blackrobe prayed.

From without the long lodge came the shoutings of the whole village, whooping and dancing, as I well knew, around the stage on which were my five condemned tribesmen.

They seemed far away and it was very peaceful to be here with my other father.

"Listen, Tarcisius, not to that, but to me," said Blackrobe, and his brown eyes seemed to shine; "sometime soon the opportunity will come for you to escape from this tiresome captivity. Take it in God's Name and know that I, like another Guardian Angel, will be with you along the last length of the trail."

I told my other father that I had dreaded the punishment of those captives who attempted to escape to our country in the north and were overtaken by our Iroquois masters. Their burning is through two whole nights and they are not released by death till the dawning of the second morning. I have been forced to see recaptured slaves of the village die and I know.

But Blackrobe corrected me: "There are other ways of escape. Soon you will know what I mean. Fear none of the dangers, for I will be close to my little one along the whole length of this narrow trail. It will end happily, for this I have asked and of this I am assured."

As he finished saying this, he put his mangled hands on my bent head and drew me down close to his breast.

Strength that I did not possess before was within my heart.

Then I made my confession and I had to leave him.

Outside of the long lodge it was already towards evening. I met White Oak and Curly Dog. I knew the meaning of this coming.

I could do nothing and my heart was heavy. All I could do was to go and station myself in the shadows across the lane from White Oak's long lodge. I kept my eyes on the bear skin that covered the entrance to the long lodge.

I had not been there many minutes when I saw the old sorcerer, White Oak, and my other father hobbling painfully at his side. A village cur came snapping at their heels.

Blackrobe was not bound. There was no need.

It was not quite dark and I saw his face clearly. It was his eyes that I noticed the most. They seemed to shine.

The two passed quite close to where I sat. My other father saw me huddled there in the shadows and without stopping he lifted his mangled right hand and then smiling directly down at me, he blessed me as he passed along.

Again the village cur came snapping and I sailed a shell and caught him in the ribs. He yelped and bounded between two long lodges. No cur of a dog was going to follow my Blackrobe. At least I could prevent that.

As I watched the two walk on, a shadow fell on me and I looked up. The evil face of Curly Dog was grinning down at me.

Ahead they had come to the entrance to White Oak's long lodge. Blackrobe in his kindly way reached for the bear skin that made the swinging door and lifted it back. It must have pained him very much to do this.

The old sorcerer, White Oak, stooped and disappeared. Then the bear skin was lifted and Blackrobe bent low to enter.

At that instant Curly Dog whipped his tomahawk from his shoulder and as the lightning flashes, hurled it through the evening air.

The shining hatchet struck my other father over the right ear and he fell forward, partly within the lodge entrance.

I heard him utter quite distinctly, "Jesus. Jesus."

He quivered and his body moved as René Goupil's had done till Curly Dog with upraised knife pounced on him. . . .

My Blackrobe had gone to God but I did not feel sad within my breast when I thought about my other father as a martyr of Christ, yet I felt very lonely—more lonely than I had all these years of my captivity. I, Tarcisius Tandihetsi, say so.

Chapter Twenty-Five

A Mangled Hand

ALL THAT NIGHT the Mohawk village was burning the five of my tribesmen. No man or squaw or child slept. I did not sleep either. Three times I tried to get into the long lodge where my other father's companion was bound. I wanted to give this Lalande the message entrusted to me. But the Iroquois guard wore the sign of the Bear Clan tattooed on his breast and he clubbed me away.

Then I had an idea. I would go outside the palisades and make my way in through the back of the long lodge. For I was very anxious to do this last favor for my Blackrobe.

No Mohawk disturbed me. They were all down by the burnings. I came to the gate that faces towards the Great Bear in the skies. It was deserted and the demon shoutings of the Iroquois were suddenly softened as I passed through the entrance to Ossernenon.

Something drew my eyes just beyond the entrance. I turned and looked up. The moon had risen and was partly above the rows of palings. Clearly in the center of this silver disc was a tall paling and affixed to it a freshly severed head.

I did not need to come closer to know whose this was. But I did come closer and stand on tiptoe.

The eyes of my Blackrobe were closed. He looked peaceful as I had seen him asleep back in my village of Teanaustayae when I was a small boy and he first became my other father by pouring Saving Waters on my forehead. It made me stronger to gaze up at

159

him, and the great longing came over me to go quickly to God and be with him again.

Then, alas! I remembered why I had come beyond the palisades and I crept along the outside palings till I came to the small passage the children used. It led into the village directly behind the long lodge where the young white brave was bound. I wiggled through. Dropping on my belly, I crept forward till I thought I was close to the captive's place.

I was right, for listening, I heard quite distinctly someone saying: "Jesu, my Jesu, all for Thee."

This I knew was Lalande. I broke off a piece of bark till I could see beyond the darkness the glowing coals of a fireplace in the center of the long lodge. I whispered to this Lalande softly: "If you can, stoop low and listen. I come from the Blackrobe."

The voice beyond the bark wall ceased to call on the Lord and I heard the movements of one turning over. He groaned, for painful must have been his every movement. I know, for I still remember those first nights after I ran the gauntlet.

"Listen. I am Tarcisius, Blackrobe's altar boy. You know who I am?"

"I know you, Tarcisius. Often has Father Jogues told me of you. Why do you court danger by coming near me now?"

"It is because Blackrobe ordered it. I may not stay long. These are the last words of Blackrobe for you."

I repeated my other father's message.

The young white brave said the words after me.

"Just a little while! I will remember the words. They are very helpful. Before you go, tell me this. What have they done to Blackrobe? The guards will not tell me."

"He was tomahawked this evening and his head is spiked to a paling beyond the northern gate at this very moment."

The voice in the dark exulted: "He has won his palm then! Blessed Father Jogues! Would that I was worthy to gain mine!"

Then the young white brave sighed and continued wearily: "But the Iroquois guard tells me my life has been spared by the council."

"They told that to Blackrobe when the Bear Clan was outvoted at the council. This clan wishes to kill all the Christians in the——"

The young white brave interrupted me to plead: "Go, Tarcisius, for Mohawks are entering now the long lodge. Go quickly."

I flattened out on the blackness of the ground and listened as the doe does in the thicket.

The young white brave was praying again in low tones.

Now beyond the bark walls I heard the soft steps of more than three Iroquois. Then there came a sharp thud. It was the same sound I had heard earlier in the evening when Blackrobe fell at the doorway of White Oak's lodge.

The voice of Lalande called: "Jesu! Jesu! Je——"

I heard another sound. It was a gasp.

All was silent beyond the bark wall. As I listened, the distant chanting and shouts came distinctly to me, especially clear were the shrill screams of the children enjoying the burnings.

I wiggled away and within my breast was not sorrow. For I knew the young white brave had gone with Blackrobe to God. He had escaped so much. I, Tarcisius Tandihetsi, say so.

There was a narrow passage between the long lodge and the inner row of the palisades. I heard growlings in the darkness ahead. There were village curs, fighting over meat.

Instead of going through the small opening in the palisades I decided to go up this long dark passage and return to my own compartment in Who Has the Face Black's lodge. On such a night as this no Huron captive's life was safe.

Just where the moonlight showed strong at the end of the narrow passage I came upon three dogs. They suddenly began to leap and snarl and snap over some prize.

I came out and straightened up in the moonlight. I put my hand to my side as though to draw a knife. The dogs well knew this gesture. Their snarls turned to yelps and they fled away.

Blackrobe's aunt, the old squaw Who Keeps the Kettle, met me as I came to my compartment. She had been weeping.

She pulled me down, and throwing a deer skin over me, ordered: "Lie there, Little Spoon, while I speak and then go. They have killed Ondesonk. He was a good man and you were dear to him."

Quickly she told me Partridge and sorcerers of the Bear Clan, in defiance of the council's ruling, had decided to burn all the Christian captives.

"Partridge is even now seeking you. Jumping Rabbit saw you the night you dug up Blackrobe's box. He followed, and this afternoon he took Partridge to the hollow tree and they found the robes for the Prayer. Partridge knows all and he will not wait to burn you over the slow fires. This the Huron squaw, Theresa, says.

"There is no time to lose. You must take to the long trail that leads north to the Great River. It is your only chance. You are a dead boy if you remain here till dawn comes."

I listened while the old squaw talked the hurried words. I remembered the words of my other father, "I will be with you on the trail," and I decided to do as Who Keeps the Kettle said. Her tongue is not split, because she liked Blackrobe.

The old squaw stopped suddenly and her hand pressed down hard against my shoulder. I lay still under the deer skin.

Presently I heard the voice of Partridge and he was demanding: "Old squaw of squaws, has that Huron puppy returned to his bed?"

Very still I lay as Blackrobe's aunt told the Iroquois to look and find out. She had a very sharp tongue. She was not afraid of any brave in Ossernenon.

All the time I heard him moving in the next compartment and when he had gone out disappointed, Who Keeps the Kettle fetched me steaming meat from the pot and this I ate, for I might not find much food on the trail.

When it was quiet beyond the long lodge, Who Keeps the Kettle brought me a bow and arrows.

I had my knife. With this I ripped off a piece of bark that covered the side wall of the long lodge and I managed to squeeze between the lodge poles.

I sought the gate that faces the Great Bear in the skies. Beyond it the dogs were growling in the moonlight. I hid till I saw there were no Iroquois by this northern gate.

As I went through, my eyes were lifted to the palings and then I had another shock. There were two heads spiked there now. The Bear Clan had been prompt in their work. One head still dripped. It could not have been placed there many minutes.

I looked up into the boyish countenance of this one and the eyes were also closed peacefully. I was suddenly sorry that I had ever been jealous of this young companion of my other father.

Gazing on the still heads I felt stronger for the hard trail and the many leagues ahead of me.

Half an arrow's flight beyond the northern gate I met more village dogs. They were fighting furiously. One dashed towards me. Two more were in pursuit.

In the moonlight I saw the first one held in his mouth what I thought was a thick piece of wood. I slashed down with my knife and the village cur dropped that which he carried. It fell and rolled at my very moccasins.

It was a mangled hand. . . .

Chapter Twenty-Six

A Palm and a Crown

AT THE SIGHT of that hand lying there in the moonlight, I knelt and picked it up. I recognized it. It was the hand that had poured Saving Waters on my forehead. I kissed it and the tears came till the heart within my breast would burst. But when I held close the still hand with the poor missing finger ends, I remembered this hand had held God and I felt strength in holding it.

Then down the trail I made out other lean village dogs and they were greedily tearing something. I ran towards them. I had to slash with my knife before the beasts would retreat.

A badly torn bit of black robe covered what was there. Brain urged me to go on, for the danger of pursuit was very close. But I listened to heart and I stooped and began to drag that body towards the dark tunnel that led down into the ravine. The lean village dogs followed, growling in their throats, but they knew enough not to come within reach of my knife.

When I reached the spot under the great oak tree where many moons ago Blackrobe and I had buried what we had recovered of René Goupil's bones, I halted. I was tired. I knew the village dogs were but waiting up the trail and I dared not leave my other father there. Down further into the ravine I went till I felt the icy waters of the creek soak my moccasins. The body floated on the black rushing waters and I guided it downstream, for I remembered the deep hole where we had weighed down René Goupil.

When I had come to where the water was up to my lungs, I stopped. This was a gentle eddy and there was no rushing current. The body floated easily. I sunk it and catching it firmly under a root, I swam ashore and sought in the blackness till I had found several heavy stones. Again and again I returned till I had these stones in place and I hoped the body of my Blackrobe was safe from the teeth of the dogs. It is not right for hungry dogs to have one who is a Martyr of Christ. I, Tarcisius Tandihetsi, say so.

As I turned away and started to wade ashore, something came bobbing up. I reached for it and it was the mangled hand that I had shoved under the body. This I clasped and brought ashore. I was very cold and my teeth were chattering.

Up the hillside out of the ravine I heard the voices of Iroquois. They were calling to one another. I recognized Partridge's voice and that of the boy, Jumping Rabbit.

I knew already the search for me had started and, like timber wolves on the trail, it would be kept up till I was run down and brought back.

Faintly came the shoutings from those who danced around the five stakes. It was not pleasant to think of what was happening to my Huron tribesmen there in the midst of the smoky slow fires.

I feared till I pressed the hand that I held and there came back to me the feeling I had always had, when I clasped that hand of my other father. It was that feeling of such safety. All at once I forgot I was crouching here in the darkness of the ravine. I was back in the canoe on the Great River that last morning of freedom and holding the nice hand of my other father. He was telling me again the story of little Isaac and the Squaw in Blue. I could even see the wooded green banks of the river and Eustace, my tall father, paddling silently. I knew if I could pierce the night and see the poor torn hand in my own, it would not be nice looking, but here in the deep shadows it seemed to be warm and tender with life.

I remembered that time my other father had told me, "The life of man is not longer than the finger of a hand" and I thought of the long cold trail to the north . . . the gray wolves that never tire . . . how the horse, "Jan," had neighed and then struggled and lay still . . . and I remembered what Blackrobe had told us Hurons when we lay on the stage, condemned to burn, "Terrible will be the torture, my brothers, but they will not last long and a glory without end will soon follow."

Suppose I did escape to my country to the north and did grow up to put wicked stains on the robe of grace that I wore on my soul and like the apostate, Snake Tooth, died that way? Then I would never go to God, never be near to my other father again, and never see the Squaw in Blue, who is so good to us Hurons.

So near to me seemed my other father and again there came the fancy that his mangled hand that I clasped was beautiful and shapely once more. I was cold and my teeth were chattering as the pebbles rattle in the sorcerer's turtle shell, but the heart within my breast was beating strong and true now.

I stood up. I had made my decision. It was the right decision for me to make. I am Tarcisius, a chief's son.

With the hand of my other father in my own, I walked up out of the dark ravine, where lay the mutilated bodies of René Goupil and Blackrobe. I walked openly in the moonlight. For I was not fleeing any more from those who hated the Prayer.

There were no Iroquois near the northern gate. Even the lean village dogs were not in sight.

I looked up to where in the darkness, for the moon had gone now, I knew the heads of two of God's Martyrs were spiked to palings. I could not see them now, but I did not need to. I felt them. Such peace and strength had come into my breast that I knew my heart was beating as steadily as Eustace, my father's, beat that last time I saw him on the stage. And as I knew my Blackrobe's heart beat when he walked by the side of the old sorcerer, White Oak, towards the long lodge a few hours ago.

When I stepped within the triple palisades of Ossernenon no Mohawk was visible, yet I knew that I walked not alone. For I felt Eustace, my father . . . René Goupil . . . Wild Berries, whom I had helped to receive Saving Waters . . . this lad Lalande, but a few years older than I . . . and my own Blackrobe himself were very near. So close were they that if I but closed my eyes I would see them encouraging me. Their presence—the presence of Martyrs of Christ—flooded me with strength. Such strength as I had never known before.

Between the long lodges of White Oak and Who Has the Face Black the wind came to my nostrils. It brought the smell of burnt flesh. I knew the war kettles were filling. For a moment I forgot those who walked unseen at my side. But I made the Sign on my forehead, breast and shoulders. I looked up beyond the bark roofs of the long lodges and I walked on steadily again.

I knew that less than an arrow's flight ahead of me I would come into the flickering lights that came from the stakes. This was "the last of the trail" and "the narrow path to Heaven" that Blackrobe meant.

A few steps. I saw the dancing mob of Iroquois; feathered braves and squaws and little children. They had not seen me yet. They were intent about the five fires. To one side stood a small group of Broad Breeches and I recognized the traders and Dirk De Witte among them. I did not know that Dirk was in Ossernenon. He alone of that cruel mob would feel sorrow when he saw me tied and suffering. He had been kind to Blackrobe and to me.

There and then I asked God that Dirk might have Saving Waters and I felt some day God would let him.

Holding fast to that mangled hand, I stepped out of the shadows of the long lodge into the uncertain lights of the square. There was a shout from the fringe of the mob and several Iroquois rushed forward to seize me.

I looked above the stakes to the east where the darkness of the night was just beginning to break. The stars had all gone to bed. It was towards dawn. And I knew when dawn came I would be with my other father . . . the Squaw in Blue . . . God.

An Epilogue

Mangled Hands is an historical story in the very best sense of the word. The outstanding facts of the lives of the heroes, Jogues, Goupil and Lalande, as well as the series of events which led them to their glorious deaths are delineated with strict regard to historical truth. Local coloring and setting are true to the colonial and missionary period in which the action takes place. *Mangled Hands* not only will delight our Catholic youth, but will be read with real relish by their elders whether or not they are familiar with the story of these heroes of God who founded the Church in America with their blood.

No writer of historical fiction has had a greater wealth of material to draw upon than that which presented itself to the author of *Mangled Hands*, ready to be woven by his skilful fingers into the absorbing story of the First American Martyrs. Father Boyton had at his disposal the seventy-one volumes of the *Jesuit Relations*.

It is a marvel that these volumes, which are a lasting monument to one of the most glorious missionary periods of the Church since apostolic days, should be so little known and appreciated by American Catholics. It is still more marvelous that the name of the heroes whose doings are recorded therein should not be household words in Catholic quarters. Protestants have not been slow to bear testimony to the deeds and heroism of the makers of the *Relations*. Bancroft said, "Not a cape was turned, not a river entered but a Jesuit led the way." Ingram Kip, Protestant Bishop of California, said of Jogues: "So died one of that glorious band that had shown greater devotion in the cause of Christianity than has ever been seen since the time of the Apostles; men whose lives and sufferings reveal a story more touching and pathetic than anything in the records of our country, and whose names should be kept in grateful remembrance; stern, high-wrought men who might have stood high in court or camp, and who could contrast their desolate state in the lowly wigwam with the refinement and affluence that waited on them in their earlier years, but who had given up home and love of kindred and the golden ties of relationship for God and man."

Of the *Relations* themselves, Reuben Gold Thwaites, then Secretary of the State Historical Society of Wisconsin, wrote in his introductory editorial essay to the Cleveland edition: "The Jesuits performed a great service to mankind in publishing their annals, which are, for historian, geographer, and ethnologist, among our first and best authorities. Many of the Relations were written in Indian camps, amid a chaos of distractions. Insects innumerable tormented the journalists, they were immersed in scenes of squalor and degradation, overcome by fatigue and lack of proper sustenance, often suffering from wounds and disease, maltreated in a hundred ways by hosts who, at times might more properly be called jailers; and not seldom had savage superstition risen to such a height, that to be seen making a memorandum was certain to arouse the ferocious enmity of the band. It is not surprising that the composition of these journals of the Jesuits is sometimes crude; the wonder is that they could be written at all. Nearly always the style is simple and direct. Never does the narrator descend to self-glorification; he never complains of his lot, but sets forth his experiences in phrases the most matter-of-fact. His meaning is seldom obscure. We gain from his pages a vivid picture of life in the primeval forests, as he lived it; we seem to see him upon his long canoe journeys, squatted amidst his dusky fellows, working his passage at the paddles, and carrying cargoes upon the portage trail: we see him the butt and scorn of the savage camp, sometimes deserted in the heart of the wilderness, and obliged to wait for another flotilla or to make his way alone as best as he can. Arrived at last at his journey's end, we often find him vainly seeking shelter in the squalid huts of the natives, with every man's hand against him, but his own heart open to them all. We find him, even when at last domiciled in some far-away village, working against hope to save the unbaptized from eternal damnation; we seem to see the rising storm of opposition, invoked by native medicine-men—who to his seventeenth century imagination seem devils indeed—and at last the bursting climax of superstitious frenzy which sweeps him and his before it. Not only do these devoted missionaries—never in any field has been witnessed greater personal heroism than theirs—live and breathe before us in the *Relations*; but we have in them our first competent account of the Red Indian at a time when relatively uncontaminated by contact with Europeans."

It is a fervent hope that novelists like Father Boyton will by further books popularize for the busy men and women of today the stories of all the heroes of the *Relations*. Certainly the story of Jogues will long linger in the minds and hearts of the readers of *Mangled Hands*. What zeal, courage, strength, meekness, and patience were united in this "Knight of Christ!" How could his frail frame stand up under the burdens put upon it: interminable journeys, coarse food, unceasing filth and disease, death ever-present in forms horrible enough to appal nerves of steel?

It is all a romance of God, and like so many of His romances is written in blood. What is most consoling to American Catholics is, that the life epic of three of the Jesuit Martyrs of North America was completed on American soil.

Between Amsterdam and Fonda in the Mohawk Valley, gateway of the West, there is an eminence that rises sharply from the sluggish waters of the Mohawk river. In the middle of the seventeenth century its height was crowned by a fortress village of the fierce Mohawks, one of the tribes of Iroquois. It was then called

Ossernenon, by its Indian name; it is now Martyrs Hill, in the confines of the village of Auriesville.

Up the slope of this eminence, Jogues and Goupil ran the gauntlet on August 14, 1642, the vigil of the feast of Our Lady's Assumption. It was on this summit that Jogues and Goupil were tortured, and here at different times Jogues, Goupil, and Lalande received the blows that reddened the soil of New York State with the blood of its first Blessed Martyrs.

What spot could be more sacred to American Catholics! Should they not treasure it above silver and gold? For the last forty years a comparatively few of the faithful have come hither as pilgrims to the blessed spot of Martyrdom. A little wooden chapel has arisen, a memorial cross has been erected, and out-door stations wind up the Hill of Prayer, where Jogues and Goupil were wont to pour forth their prayers and tears. Here, too, as many ex-voto offerings show, there have been wonderful outpourings of grace, favors granted, cures wrought. But for all that, the story of the Martyrs and their shrine is unknown to the vast bulk of American Catholics. May the day come when they will show for God's blessed dead the same zeal they manifest for our country's heroes, and erect on Martyrs Hill a fitting memorial to the Knights of Christ whose blood has been the seed of the Church in America.

IGNATIUS W. COX, S.J.,
Editor of the Pilgrim

MEMORIAL DAY, 1926.

"MANGLED HANDS"

A Story of the New York Martyrs

By NEIL BOYTON, S.J.

Benziger Brothers: Net, $1.25

If the individual life of each saint were written in the style and with the naturalness and vigor of this narrative, it would indeed prove to be a "best seller" among our American boys and girls.

So thrilling are the exploits vividly related, and so enormous is the fund of Indian habits and customs bound up in this story, that the reader will have difficulty in making himself realize that he is not one of the Huron tribe. What makes the tale still more gripping is the fact that it is related by the youngest of the Martyrs, Tarcisius (formerly Little Spoon) Tandihetsi, 12-year-old son of a Huron chieftain and proud of it. In his own quaint language, he conducts us on the fatal trip with his warriors and Missionaries. The band is ambushed, a battle with arrows and rifles ensues and all are killed or captured. While enjoying a hair-raising Indian story, the reader will be unconsciously absorbing the actual details of the martyrdom of Blessed Isaac Jogues and companions, Jesuits, the first Martyrs of the United States.

BOOK REVIEW FROM *THE HEIGHTS*, MAY 17, 1927

ALSO BY FR. BOYTON

View a sample chapter from each title at www.staidanpress.com.

REDROBES

Thirteen-year-old orphan Jacques gets into trouble in Quebec, and decides to run away to Huronia and become an interpreter for his Jesuit guardian, Father John Brebeuf. But his journey along the Iroquois-infested river may not be so easy as he hopes!

$17.00 — 300 pages. Available at amazon.com.

OTHER TITLES AVAILABLE FROM ST. AIDAN PRESS

THE QUEEN'S TRAGEDY, by Msgr. Robert Hugh Benson

"Upon the publication of former books of mine several kindly critics remarked that the reign of Mary Tudor told a very different story with regard to the Catholic character. It is that story which I am now attempting to set forth as honestly as I can."

$19.00 — 364 pages. Available at amazon.com.

THE NET, by Agnes Blundell

"Roger felt a freezing dew break out upon his forehead. The net was over him it seemed; in vain he told himself that he could establish his identity. His head was worth forty pounds to the vile creatures at the stair foot, and once in their clutches who knew if he could ever communicate with his friends?"

$16.00 — 264 pages. Available at amazon.com.

THEY MET ROBIN HOOD, by Agnes Blundell

Osmund does a good turn to one of Robin Hood's outlaws and makes friends with the band. But how can outlaws help his family against a friend of Prince John?

$15.00 — 214 pages. Available at amazon.com.

THE ANCHORHOLD, by Enid Dinnis

A chaplain's sermon drove Editha de Beauville to give up the world and enter the religious life. But could a strong-willed noblewoman accept and embrace full seclusion in an anchorhold? Read on to learn how she fared, and how her life affected those around her: Sir Aleric, her erstwhile suitor, now a crusader knight; Fr. Nicholas, a young priest who was quite bright, and thought so too; and Fiddlemee, the witty yet wise court jester whose past held a surprising secret.

$14.00 — 196 pages. Available at amazon.com.

THE ROAD TO SOMEWHERE, by Enid Dinnis

Richard and Ann discover a real Tudor house in London being sold cheap, complete with leather latch-strings, a tale of hidden treasure, and a wonderful piper. But the treasure turns out to be an old altar-stone. Will it lose them the house and each other, or set them on the real road to Somewhere?

$10.00 — 106 pages. Available at amazon.com.

THE SHEPHERD OF WEEPINGWOLD, by Enid Dinnis

Sir Robert Luffkyn, rich grandson of a peasant, has purchased the manor of Weepingwold from the noble but impoverished de Lessels, intending to make the renamed Luffkynwold a busy center of his tanning trade. He sends Petronilla, last de Lessels, to Gracerood, intending her for its future Abbess, and plucks little Brother Kit from the cloister to become the new parson of the long-abandoned church. How will Father Kit fare with the parish and his own soul? Will Petronilla find her true vocation? And is there really a witch in the parish?

$14.00 — 202 pages. Available at amazon.com.

SCOUTING FOR SECRET SERVICE, by Fr. Bernard F. J. Dooley

Frank and George are going to spend their summer vacation in the Adirondacks, thanks to Frank's uncle Ed. But once they get there, they realize something fishy is going on. Can they trust Pete, their Indian guide, or is he mixed up in it too? And is Frank's mysterious uncle really behind it all?

$14.00 — 188 pages. Available at amazon.com.

THE COMING OF THE MONSTER, by Fr. Owen Francis Dudley

The Masterful Monk returns to England to fight against the Bolshevik cause, to find beautiful, idealistic Verna Wray torn between her family's wealth and her French Catholic suitor. But how much suffering is Red hate still to cause them all?

$15.00 — 218 pages. Available at amazon.com.

THE MASTERFUL MONK, by Fr. Owen Francis Dudley

Brother Anselm comes back to England to counter the Atheist's efforts to destroy the influence of Catholic morals. Between his lectures he is drawn into a struggle for the soul of Beauty Dethier, who is Catholic but fascinated by the "freedom" of the world and the Atheist. It will take more than argument to save her from disaster.

$18.00 — 342 pages. Available at amazon.com.

WILL MEN BE LIKE GODS? & THE SHADOW ON THE EARTH, by Fr. Owen Francis Dudley

Father Dudley's first two books on human happiness are published together here—his rare collection of essays together with the novel which introduces his most famous character, the Masterful Monk.

$15.00 — 216 pages. Available at amazon.com

CANDLELIGHT ATTIC AND ODD JOB'S, by Cecily Hallack

Here are seven true stories in honour of the Seven Joys of Our Blessed Lady, and ten more invented ones about the delightful Barnabas Job, to make a comfortable book for those who are afraid of the dark.

$14.00 — 192 pages. Available at amazon.com.

THE HAPPINESS OF FATHER HAPPÉ, by Cecily Hallack

Shingle Bay did not know what to make of Fr. Savinius Happé. He was a cheerful, rotund Franciscan, a famous author of books on everything from Etruscan civilization to Alpine meadows to beetles, and someone who had never quite mastered the English language. His jovial demeanor concealed a wisdom that alternately bewildered, astonished, but ultimately won over the people of Shingle Bay.

$10.00 — 112 pages. Available at amazon.com.

THREE RELIGIOUS REBELS, by M. Raymond, O.C.S.O.

"There must be men who give themselves to God, because there is a God who gave Himself to man." This is the story of three such men—St. Robert of Molesme, St. Alberic, and St. Stephen Harding.

$17.00 — 294 pages. Available at amazon.com.

THE RED INN OF SAINT LYPHAR, by Anna T. Sadlier

Once Saint Lyphar was a happy village in France, ruled by a generous Marquis and taught by the good Curé. Now the Révolution has put the

Curé to death, and the villagers are about to rise under the famous leader Jambe d'Argent. But a Revolutionary spy is lurking near the Inn....

$13.00 — 168 pages. Available at amazon.com.

CON OF MISTY MOUNTAIN, by Mary T. Waggaman

"It had been a long night for Con. Just what had happened to him he was at first too dazed to know. Dennis had flung him into the smoking-room with no very gentle hand, turned the key and left him to himself. And, sinking down dully upon a rug that felt very soft and warm after the hard flight over the mountain, Con was glad to rest his bruised, aching limbs, his dizzy head, without any thought of what was to come upon him next."

$14.00 — 190 pages. Available at amazon.com.

NON-FICTION

THE AMERICAN HERESY, by Christopher Hollis.

The history of Jeffersonian America and of its downfall is told here in the lives of four famous statesmen: Thomas Jefferson, John C. Calhoun, Abraham Lincoln, and Woodrow Wilson.

$18.00 — 358 pages. Available at amazon.com.

THE STORY OF THE WAR IN LA VENDÉE AND THE LITTLE CHOUAN-NERIE, by George J. Hill, M.A.

The story of the brave French Catholics who rose up in arms against the revolutionary government.

$18.00 — 342 pages. Available at amazon.com.

CATHOLICISM AND SCOTLAND, by Compton Mackenzie

The little known history of the Scots who sought to defend their country and their Faith from the onslaught of Protestantism.

$12.00 — 138 pages. Available at amazon.com.

DOMINICAN SAINTS, by the Novices of the Dominican House of Studies

The astonishing lives of fourteen saints of the Dominican Order.

$19.00 — 392 pages. Available at amazon.com.